THE QUEST FOR
THE SILVER CASTLE

Tales of the King, Book One

THE QUEST FOR THE SILVER CASTLE

LELA GILBERT

ILLUSTRATED BY BEVERLY BURGE

Wolgemuth & Hyatt, Publishers, Inc.
Brentwood, Tennessee

The mission of Wolgemuth & Hyatt, Publishers, Inc. is to publish and distribute books that lead individuals toward:

- A personal faith in the one true God: Father, Son, and Holy Spirit;

- A lifestyle of practical discipleship; and

- A worldview that is consistent with the historic, Christian faith.

Moreover, the Company endeavors to accomplish this mission at a reasonable profit and in a manner which glorifies God and serves His Kingdom.

Wolgemuth & Hyatt, Publishers, Inc.
1749 Mallory Lane, Suite 110
Brentwood, Tennessee 37027

Library of Congress Cataloging-in-Publication Data

Gilbert, Lela.
   The quest for the silver castle / Lela Gilbert.
      p. cm. — (Tales of the king ; book 1)
   Summary: In a land whose law is "Love the king," a girl questions how she can feel love for a king she's never seen, and her adventurous search for understanding involving a long journey and a struggle against six cruel kings provides a parallel with one's personal striving for faith that God exists.
   ISBN 1-56121-069-2
   [1. Kings, queens, rulers, etc.—Fiction. 2. Adventure an adventurers—Fiction. 3. Parables.] I. Title. II. Series: Gilbert, Lela. Tales of the king ; book 1.
PZ7.G3748Qu 1991
[Fic]—dc20   91-17085
                                                                       CIP
                                                                        AC

For Dylan and Colin,
With My Love.

With Sincere Gratitude
To David Aikman.

CONTENTS

ONE

THE LAW
OF THE LAND

nce there was a kingdom. And in the kingdom was a tiny, peaceful village. And in the village was a girl with wide, brown eyes, soft with dreams. Her name was Theodora.

The village where Theodora lived was much like every other village in the kingdom. You or I might have confused it with dozens of other little communities of much the same size. But Theodora had never lived anywhere else. In fact, she had never been anywhere else. She knew by heart every high road and house and hiding place in her village. And she thought it was the most wonderful place to live in all the world.

The main street of the village was called Castle Street. It was a narrow lane of well-worn stones, flanked on the east side by neat and all-but-identical shops—the butchery, the chemist's shop, the green-grocery, the bakery, and the sweets shop where fathers bought newspapers (or the newspaper shop where children bought sweets).

On the west side of Castle Street were a small and simple inn, a post office, and a friendly looking building with a faded wooden sign that read *The King's Warrior*.

After a hard day's work, the village men would gather there at twilight to sing and laugh and forget the fact that tomorrow's rising sun would bring today's chores around once again.

South of the shops and the inn and the post office and the gathering place, Castle Street grew a little wider, crossed a bridge that spanned the Seabound River, and disappeared into a dark, ancient wood. Theodora had no idea where the road beyond the wood might lead.

To the north of the village, the road began to curve, winding past farmlands that spread across the hills like a large, green quilt. On every farm was a humble, white-washed cottage. And on every hill was a stone-fenced field, dotted with a flock of sheep or striped with an orchard.

Come summer, even the homeliest cottages wore skirts of brilliant flower gardens, bright with every shade of purple and crimson and blue and sun yellow. Come winter, pale silver snows and glistening icicles made all things beautiful.

Theodora often left her own cottage, which she shared with her mother and her father and her brothers and her sisters, and walked north on the widening road to the small apple grove where the road forked. One part of the road led to a larger township and, after that, to the City of Bells, the largest city in all the kingdom.

The other part of the road grew narrow and winding and began to climb upward, past the quiet, sloping pastures, past the higher, forested hills. Soon the road disappeared forever into the treacherous mountains that towered above the valley.

In those mountains was the marvelous sight that gave the tiny village its name, Place-Beneath-the-Castle. From any point in the village—Theodora's cottage, Castle Street, the Seabound River Bridge, or the apple grove—it could be seen. The castle was built high on the highest pinnacle of the highest mountain in the kingdom. Admittedly, often as not, it looked more like a bank of clouds, a dazzling rainbow, or a sapphire shimmering in the blue sky than like a real castle. Its turrets seemed to fade in and out of view. And, on wind-chilled autumn mornings, wood smoke from cottage fires and leaf smoke from the orchards hid the mountains and the castle completely. (Still, the fragrance in the air and the crispness of the autumn wind were so delightful that, for an hour or two, Theodora didn't really care if the castle vanished or not, at least temporarily.)

Many of the villagers didn't actually believe that the castle was there at all. True, some of the children were sure they could see it; and some of the young couples vowed they had watched it by moonlight; and some of the mothers swore that the castle had been ever so clearly in sight when their babies were fresh born and warm in their arms. And naturally the oldest people, their eyes misted with years, stated with passion that they could see it best.

But, for the most part, the villagers explained the castle away. It was an illusion, they said, brought on by gathering storms or cavorting rain showers or too much summer sun. Or perhaps it was simply whimsy. And a handful of the most stern-faced villagers even said that the castle was an unforgivable lie. So, although the real name of Theodora's village was Place-Beneath-the-Castle, the villagers simply called it Place.

From the time she could first understand, Theodora knew that there were rules in Place. There were rules about stealing from the shops and telling lies and fighting. And there were even grim, frightening rules about hurting and killing, although nothing like that had happened in Place for hundreds of years.

But besides the village rules, there was another law in the kingdom. It was carved on the shining gold and silver coins. It rippled on the scarlet flag that flew outside the post office. And it was the correct answer to the schoolroom question "What is the law of the land?"

The law was: *"Love the King."*

Generally, the villagers ignored this law. They were too busy ploughing fields, tending sheep, keeping shop, or cleaning house even to think about the King. And besides that, the King was supposed to live in the castle above the village. If there really was no castle, how could there really be a King?

Theodora was quite sure there *was* a castle. And, since there was a castle and she was certain she had seen it, she often thought and dreamed and wondered about the King who lived there. And she was forever confused by the words on the coins and the flag and the teachers' lips—*"Love the King."*

Theodora loved her quiet father more than anyone else in the world, if the truth were known. He said little to her, but she loved the lines of laughter around his eyes and the way he smiled when she told him about her imaginings.

She loved her mother, too, and often noticed the gentle way she cared for the smaller children and how she always kept wildflowers on the rough, oak table where the family shared its meals.

Theodora loved most of her sisters all of the time and all of her brothers most of the time. And she loved the animals the family kept, some for pleasure and some for food.

In a different way, she loved her friends and her teacher at the wooden schoolhouse. In yet another way, she loved the sound of rain upon the apple leaves, the smell of the fields in the hot summer sun, and the feel of snowflakes stinging her face in the December wind.

But how could she love the King?

Even though she was fairly sure there was a castle, and she was nearly sure the King lived there, the fact was that Theodora had never seen him. And as far as she knew, he had never seen her. And even though she felt a kind of stirring when she looked at the tall turrets that danced between the clouds or shined among the rainbows or glimmered in the sun-scorched sky, she couldn't really say she loved the castle. And she was absolutely sure she didn't love the King.

And yet the law of the land was *"Love the King."* Was she breaking the law?

When she asked her father, he stared gravely into her eyes for a moment and then looked away without saying a word. When she asked her mother, her mother said, "Ask your father." Theodora didn't dare ask her brothers and sisters, for they said she thought too much and dreamed too many dreams and wondered about too many things.

Still, the question lingered in her mind, from the days of the winter hearth until the fields were fresh with spring. One afternoon, Theodora left the house and headed straight for the apple grove by the fork in the road. From her favorite hiding place there, she stared at the castle, rippling with rainbows. And she thought and she dreamed and she wondered.

At last she spoke out loud—so suddenly that her own words made her jump with surprise. "If you're really the King, and I'm really supposed to love you, then why don't you tell me how?"

At about that time, a young couple approached Theodora. Arm in arm, they were walking toward Place from somewhere up the road. Since she didn't know them and had nothing to lose by asking, Theodora skipped out from her hiding place and ran after the lovers. They turned and saw a small peasant child smiling at them, her wide, brown eyes soft with dreams.

"How can I love the King?" she blurted out.

"How can you what?" the young man laughed.

"How can I love the King? The law of the land says *"Love the King."* How can I love him?"

"Lovers love with their hearts," the young woman answered, looking at the man with great fondness in her eyes. The lovers' smiles left Theodora feeling that she had all at once become invisible.

She spoke quickly. "My heart beats and flutters when I'm happy or frightened, but how can I *love* with my heart?"

"Your heart is the part of you that feels," the young man said. "To love with your heart is to *feel.*" And with those words, the young couple laughed and kissed and went on their way.

Theodora walked slowly back to her hiding place, where she thought and dreamed and wondered.

A little later, a man with a peaceful smile on his face came walking, carrying a strange looking musical instrument in his arms. He plucked it and sang a song as he ambled along.

Maybe he *knows,* Theodora thought as she ran after him. "Sir," she began, "how can I love the King?"

"Love is forever sought by the soul." The minstrel seemed to be speaking only to himself. ". . . And to live without love is to never be whole."

"What is a soul?" Theodora persisted, her clear young voice bringing the man back to reality.

"There is a knowing within you," the man answered softly, looking into the upturned face before him. "Have you ever known need in a friend without being told? Have you ever known about a coming rain on a sunny day? Have you ever known your world was about to change when no change could yet be found?"

Theodora nodded uncertainly.

"Love, too, is of the soul. And to love with your soul is to *know.*" With that, the minstrel strolled on, humming as he went.

Back in her hiding place beneath the apple tree, Theodora thought and she dreamed and she wondered some more.

Just as she was about to run home with a thousand more questions in her mind, she saw a well-dressed woman riding toward her on horseback. The woman had

strapped several books to her horse's saddle and wore a
wise look upon her face.

"She looks as if she might have come from the City
of Bells," Theodora whispered to herself. "She will
surely know!"

By now, Theodora felt more courageous about asking her questions. "How can I love the King?" she de-
manded of the woman without a moment's hesitation.

"The *King?*" The woman laughed a little too loudly as
she said the word *king.* "I don't know about loving the
King, dear" (again the word sounded a little foolish), "but
to love anyone, you must use your mind. By using your
mind, you will understand the person you seek to love;
and by understanding him, you will be able to love him."

"Understand the King . . . ?"

"To love with the mind is to *understand,*" the
woman stated very emphatically. And she rode away
quickly.

Feeling somehow a little hurt, yet not knowing why,
Theodora ran home. She walked into the familiar, sup-
per-scented house in an odd mood, lost in thought.

Her father watched her as she sat gazing into the
golden fire. He reached for her, picked her up in his
strong arms, and sat her on his lap.

"Theodora, what has put those puzzles in your eyes?"

"Father," she whispered, "I talked out loud to the King,
even though he wasn't there, and I asked questions of
strangers, even though I didn't know their names."

A shadow crossed her father's face. "And what did
you learn, little one?"

"I learned that to love the King, I must love with my
heart, and I must love with my soul, and I must love

"Sir," she began, "how can I love the King?"

with my mind. But my heart doesn't feel and my soul doesn't know; and, Father, I don't understand at all!" Theodora began to cry. And when she looked into her father's face, searching for answers, he turned away. Tears welled in his eyes, too.

"Theodora," he responded at last, "you can't love someone you have never met, someone you know nothing about."

"I know, Father, but how can I meet him?"

"You'll just have to find people who say they know him and talk to them."

"Father, do *you* believe there is a King?" She whispered the next question. "Do *you* know him?"

Her father sighed wearily. "I haven't even thought about the King for a long, long time, little one."

Theodora spoke quietly and firmly. "I want to keep the law. I want to love the King."

Her father paused for several minutes before he spoke, puffing on his pipe. He chose his next words with great care. "If you want to love him, you'll have to know him. You'll have to long for him and reach for him and search for him with all your might. Once you've done that, you can then decide for yourself whether there really is a King, and if you will love him or if you will not."

With those words, he kissed her affectionately on the forehead; smoothed her long, breeze-blown hair; and set her small, brown feet back on the cottage floor.

Theodora walked back to her own safe spot by the crackling fire. She sat down, crossed her legs, and began to watch the dancing, darting flames. And she thought and she dreamed and she wondered.

TWO

THEODORA AND THE EMERALD EYE

oft, fragrant rain was tapping on the cottage window when Theodora awoke. She lay still and cozy for a moment or two, trying to shake the sleepy mist from her mind. Then, with a surge of excitement, she remembered—today was the day she would begin her search for people who knew the King!

She rose quietly because the other children were still sleeping. She pulled on her dress and her pinafore and her stockings. She tied her shoes and tiptoed into the kitchen, where her mother was already busy. Theodora picked up the tall, wooden broom and began to sweep the cottage floor. If she hurried with her morning chores, there would be more hours left in the day for her quest.

The sun was just peeking through the clouds when Theodora stepped out the door of the cottage, her housework finally completed. Ripples of excitement sent her running down the road. Then, all at once, she stopped short. "I don't know where I'm going!" She

11

laughed aloud. "How will I ever find someone who
knows the King?"

A workman was bicycling toward her, and within a
moment's time, she met up with him. He smiled, his
cheeks rosy with the brisk air, and touched his flat-billed
cap. She noticed that his eyes sparkled green as emeralds. "Morning, missy," he greeted her, still pedaling.

"Sir, I'm looking for someone who knows about the
King." Theodora turned her head, speaking quickly to
get in her question before he passed.

The workman braked his bicycle and turned to stare
at her. "Someone who knows about the King?" he repeated softly. "Why, I know about the King, missy."

"Have you met him? What is he like? Is he really in
the castle? Is there really a castle? Do you love him?"
Questions spilled out and tumbled over each other so
quickly that Theodora could hardly remember what she
had asked once she had finished asking.

"Do you know the Cloudwarren farm?"

"Yes, of course," Theodora replied impatiently. "But
what about the King?"

"Come 'round the Cloudwarren farm about noon,
and we'll have a little chat. You'll find me in the north
field. I'll be having my lunch about then." The workman
touched his hat, nodded his head, and pedaled away,
whistling as he went.

Theodora was wonderfully pleased at the prospect of
having a talk about the King. But noon seemed such a
long while away. What would she do until then? She felt
sure she simply couldn't wait! She decided to return to
the apple grove by the crossroads to watch the castle
until a better idea came along.

Stepping into the grove, she noticed that the leaves on the apple trees were still jeweled with raindrops. There was a rich, earthy scent in the air, and the sun teased plumes of vapor from the damp soil. Theodora sat on her favorite rock, put her head in her hands, and settled down to think and dream and wonder.

But, for some reason, she was having trouble concentrating. The castle looked more like a cloudbank than ever, and her mind wandered from the scent in the air to the water on the tree leaves. She noticed how a sunbeam passing through a single drop of rain looked red, then orange, then yellow, then green, then blue, then violet, then red again. She moved her head a little to make the colors change—violet to blue, blue to green, green to yellow . . . Her eyes were growing heavy when suddenly she sensed that she was no longer alone.

Theodora looked up and gasped. Standing right in front of her was a person made up of all the colors of the sun in the raindrop. He shimmered with light. His whole body seemed wrapped in rainbows. Though he had a face with two eyes, a nose, and a mouth just like hers, he seemed transparent. Theodora felt as though she was looking right through him. His expression told her that he was friendly, but still Theodora trembled with fear.

"You want to love the King," the rainbow person declared. The sound of his voice reminded Theodora of the Seabound River rushing over rocks.

"The King has heard about your search for people who know of him. He is pleased with you, Theodora. He has sent me to give you a message."

"How do you know my name?" Theodora inquired weakly.

The shimmering seemed to grow brighter when the being smiled at her. "The King knows a great deal more than your name, little one."

"What is the message?" By now her words were barely audible. With half her heart, she wished that the glistening, gleaming person would go away. With the other half, she longed for him never, ever to leave.

"Here is the message I bring to you. Ask, then open your hand to receive. Look for something, then open your eyes to discover. Visit the homes of strangers and expect to be welcomed into rooms you've never seen before.

"And, Theodora, remember. The King feels. And the King knows. And the King understands."

With those words, the being stepped back, the shimmering grew faint, and Theodora was alone once again, watching a sunbeam passing through a single drop of rain.

Her mind raced forward and stopped, flew upward and fell back. Her hands grew warm and then cold. Her legs felt as if they might melt into the earth if she tried to stand. Theodora smiled in spite of herself when she recalled how her brothers and sisters always told her that she thought too much and dreamed too many dreams and wondered about too many things.

Could she ever have imagined such a talking rainbow?

Could she possibly have dreamed his amazing words?

"Ask, then hold out your hand to receive. . . ." Ask who? Ask for what?

"Look for something, then open your eyes to discover. . . ." That made a little more sense—she was looking for people who knew about the King.

"Visit the homes of strangers . . ." Well, that was
bound to happen. No one she knew would even talk
about the King. She would have to visit strangers!

But then came the words Theodora liked best. *"The
King feels. The King knows. The King understands."*
Could that mean that the King felt and knew and understood about her, Theodora? After all, the rainbow messenger had known her name! And he also had known
that she was looking for people who would tell her
about the King.

What had her father said the night before? It
seemed almost the same message, yet it was somehow
different. She thought about the sadness in his face as
they'd talked. Why did he grow so sorrowful when he
talked about the King?

All at once, Theodora jumped to her feet. The sun
was high in the sky! How could the morning have passed
so quickly? She would have to fly like the wind to reach
the Cloudwarren farm by noon.

She left the road and raced across familiar fields toward the third white cottage to the east. She could see
the workman sitting under a tree in the distant north
field. Running and rustling through tall grass, she
reached his side at last.

She had forgotten how green his eyes were. They
sparkled with light when he looked up and smiled at
her. "Hello, missy! I wasn't sure if you'd remember to
come and visit with me."

"Oh, no, I didn't forget, sir. It's just that . . ." Words
failed Theodora at this point. She longed to ask the
green-eyed man about the rainbow being, but she was

afraid he'd think she was a liar, or worse yet, a child who didn't know fact from fantasy.

"Tell me about the King, please," Theodora begged.

And so he began his tale.

"When I was a boy," the workman began with a smile, "I wasn't as free a child as you. I could hear the birds singing in the summer. I could feel the spring rain on my face. I could smell the roses and carnations and lilies of the valley in my mother's garden. But I could see nothing. My eyes were blind to all but shadows.

"Then, one day, a stranger came to our home and asked for supper. My mother fed him and gave him fresh milk to drink. And as he sat by our fire in the evening, he lifted me onto his knee.

"'Do you love the King?' the man asked me.

"Of course, I said yes. What would any child answer? But, for some reason, he asked me again, in a different way. 'Son, do you *love* the King?'

"'I don't know the King,' I answered, quite truthfully. I didn't at the time, you know, missy."

"My problem exactly," Theodora whispered, mostly to herself.

The workman continued his story. "'The King knows about you, little boy,' said the man, 'and he's very sorry that you cannot see. He wants to help you. Do you want his help?'

"Now, missy, I'd never even thought about being able to see. There wasn't a hope in the world for such a thing. But, of course, I said yes just to be polite.

"'All right, then, lad,' he replied. 'Meet me at the crossroads tomorrow at first light.' Once I promised, he

thanked my mother for dinner, excused himself, and
went on his way.

"'What should I do?' I asked my mother after he left.

"'Do what the man said,' she replied. 'What harm
can it do?'

"Since night was no different from day to me, and
I'd been to the crossroads a thousand times before, I
found my way there before a trace of sunrise brightened
the sky. I sat down on a rock and waited, wondering
how I would know when first light had come. As the
minutes passed, I became more and more sure that the
whole thing was a cruel joke.

"Just then, I heard a voice. 'Hello, son, I see that you
are an obedient child. And I have a gift for you from the
King.' His voice sounded different, like rushing waters.

"The man placed something in my hand. At first, it
felt cool and smooth to the touch. But as I held it, it
warmed in my hand; and as it warmed, the shadows
began to clear from my eyes like cobwebs being swept
away. Soon I could see the man standing before me. He
was the first person I had ever seen! He shimmered
with color and shined like a rainbow . . . ."

Theodora caught her breath with wonder, and her
face grew pink with excitement.

". . . And when I looked in my hand, I saw what he had
placed there—an emerald eye set in an orb of crystal.

"All around us were trees and fences, and by the
dawn's light, I could see the castle shining pure as silver
on the top of the highest mountain.

"I ran all the way home. I had to close my eyes to
find my way, the sights around me were so confusing. I
ran into the house, searching for my mother. What a

strange sight she was—so dull looking, so brown, like a dusty sparrow. The sight of the King's messenger had dazzled me. It took days for me to realize that the dreary appearance of ordinary people was normal, and that the messenger was someone far, far different.

"Stranger yet, my mother said that when the man was visiting our home, he looked just like any other man—no shimmering, no rainbows, no waterfalls in his voice. I have since learned that the King's messengers take many forms."

Chills quivered in Theodora's back, her head felt tingly, and she shivered three times in a row. The workman's story had to be true. But still . . .

Before she could speak, the workman reached inside his shirt collar and pulled out a tarnished, dirty chain. Suspended on the end was a crystal orb. And inside the orb was a gloriously brilliant emerald, cut and faceted and carved in the shape of an eye. The light from it was so blinding that Theodora had to look away and blink and shade her eyes in order to see it at all.

When she looked back at the workman's face, she noticed his peaceful smile and his eyes shining green as the emerald. "Do you believe me, missy?" he asked.

"Yes," Theodora whispered, "I believe you. You see, I just saw one of the rainbow messengers myself. Do *you* believe *me?*"

The workman's green eyes glimmered with tears. "You are one of the King's children then, aren't you?"

"What do you mean?"

"If you haven't learned yet, you will soon."

The workman kissed Theodora's hand, helped her to her feet, and sent her on her way with a warning.

*Before she could speak, the workman reached inside his
shirt collar and pulled out a tarnished, dirty chain.*

"Watch out for the Children of the South. They are sent from the Six Cruel Kings. They will try to hinder you, but they will not be allowed to harm you.

"Farewell, missy. And love the King."

CHREE

FRIENDS
AND FOES

Theodora didn't see the billowing white and silver clouds that tumbled over each other as they made their way across the gleaming sky. She didn't even notice that the buds on the fruit trees were beginning to open, their sweet fragrance blending with the smell of the wet earth. She wandered away from the workman with a dazed expression on her face.

All Theodora could think about were the rainbow messenger and the workman's mysterious words. Was she really one of the King's children? Who were the Children of the South? And his last words rang loudest in her ears.

"Farewell, missy. And love the King." If she hadn't been so fascinated, she would have felt altogether frustrated. Love the King! Well, that's what her search was all about! That's what had begun her day's strange and wonderful adventure. Love the King, indeed! How she wished she knew how.

Theodora wandered aimlessly from field to field, past houses and barns and work sheds. Feeling a little weary and weak, she finally stopped to rest atop a big rock. Cows called sadly to one another as they grazed

21

the daisy-strewn pastures. Theodora's toes made circles
in the damp soil at her feet.

How can I love the King?

All at once she heard her name drifting faintly across
the fields. "Theodora!" She looked around, expecting another miracle. But alas, there was no rainbow messenger, and no green-eyed workman appeared on the horizon with more remarkable stories. Instead, she saw her
sister Beatrice shouting and waving. "I didn't realize I
was so close to home," she told herself.

A little irritated by the interruption, she shouted,
"What do you want?"

"Mother needs you!"

Theodora skipped toward her cottage, which really
was quite nearby.

"Theodora!" Her mother frowned a little when her
pink-cheeked daughter appeared in the doorway.
"Where have you been, child? Today is cleaning day, remember? And I need your help."

"Sorry, Mother. I forgot. What do you want me to do?"

"Start with the pantry. Take everything out. Wash
the shelves, the floor, and the walls. Then replace everything once you've finished. That's a good place to begin."

"Oh, Mother!" she burst out. "That will take forever!"

"Theodora," Mother responded sharply, "you have
nothing better to do than help your sisters and me with
the annual cleaning."

*Nothing is more important than finding out about
the King,* Theodora thought. But knowing better than to
answer back, Theodora bit her lip and busied herself
with the task at hand. She worked feverishly, moving the
foods to the kitchen table. She scoured the shelves and

the walls with a soapy cloth. She wiped them off and then used a coarse brush to scrub the floor.

The pantry project was far more difficult than it should have been. Two of Theodora's tiniest sisters were supposed to be helping her, but one of them sat in the middle of the pantry floor, playing with a kitten, and the other one kept washing the shelves that Theodora had already dried. Theodora found herself speaking to both of them in the most unfriendly way. At last, she shouted, "You are both useless helpers! Why don't you just get out of my way!"

And so they did.

Once everything was dry and smelled fresh and sweet, Theodora replaced the foods and announced to her mother, "I'm finished with the pantry!" At last she could get back to her search.

"Good, Theodora. Now you can begin with the clothing."

"The clothing?" Tears stung Theodora's brown eyes, and anger surged inside her.

"Yes, the clothing. Help Beatrice and Geraldine with the clothes. Sort out the ones that are too worn to repair. Make a pile of good ones that are too small for the smallest children and another pile of the good ones that need mending."

By now poor Theodora was sobbing quietly to herself, wiping her tears on her sleeve as she worked. And, sad to say, she often spoke in a snippy, snappy voice to her sisters. She refused even to look at her mother.

Her mind was darkened with disappointment. In the midst of such menial tasks, it seemed that the rainbow messenger and the green-eyed workman had appeared years before, not that very morning. In fact, at times during the endless afternoon, it almost seemed to Theodora that she had imagined everything—waterfall voices, emeralds, and all.

Once the clothes were sorted, Theodora thought for sure that she could run back outside and get on with her adventure. "Mother, is that all you need?" She tried to smile a little when she asked the question, hoping to make up for her impatient feelings. She just wished her eyes weren't so red or her cheeks so smudged.

"Well, yes, Theodora, except for one thing . . ."

"What!" The little girl's loud voice conveyed her annoyance.

Her mother turned away. "Never mind, dear. I'll ask Beatrice, instead. I can see that you don't want to be bothered." Did she detect tears in Mother's eyes, too?

Theodora was immediately sorry. "What, Mother? Just tell me."

"Theodora, I have some good news for you. You are soon to have a new brother or sister. But because of that, I'm not feeling my best at the moment. I just wanted someone to help me hang out the laundry." She put her hands on her daughter's tense shoulders. "Child, why are you so unhappy today?" She brushed back Theodora's long hair with a kind hand.

"Mother, I'll hang up the laundry, but then can I go? I want to get back to something I was doing this morning, that's all."

"What were you doing?"

"I was . . . Oh, Mother, it was nothing, really. Where are the clean clothes? I'll hang them up."

Colorful dresses and trousers and skirts and shirts snapped in the late afternoon breeze as quickly as Theodora pinned them up on the line. The sun was not far from the horizon, and Theodora felt a surge of joy. Once the last clothespin was in place and the basket returned to the kitchen, she ran like the wind, getting away from the house as fast as she could go. Once out of sight, she slowed her steps, and with a great sense of freedom, she began to wander from field to field once again.

She sat down on the steps of an old, whitewashed outbuilding on a nearby farm.

How can I love the King?

She remembered the gentle, dear faces of the people she really loved and felt guilty for her unpleasant behavior at home. How did she show them she loved them?

Sometimes she ran up to her mother and threw her arms around her, burying her face in clean smelling, faded skirts. Sometimes she held her father's warm face in her hands and kissed his scratchy, tired cheeks. Sometimes she lifted a little brother onto her lap or walked hand in hand with an older sister. But how could she love the King? She couldn't very well do any of those things to him. She couldn't even see him!

All at once Theodora became aware of a sound behind her. She jumped a little, startled by the soft thump, thump, thump of wood against wood. When she turned to look, she met the merry gaze of a very old woman who sat churning butter just inside the door of the whitewashed little shed.

Theodora felt a flutter of fear. The woman was dappled with sunlight, and leaf shadows played games with

Theodora's eyes as she tried to see what the stranger looked like. The old lady wore a brown, homespun dress. Her hair was streaked, brown with silver. She smiled warmly and toothlessly at Theodora.

"You seem to be thinking very carefully, little girl."

"Oh . . . yes, I suppose I was." Theodora felt a bit embarrassed. Then a burst of courage strengthened her heart, and she managed to ask the old woman the question she'd repeated so many times in the past few days.

"Do you . . ." she barely breathed the words. "Do you know the King?"

The old woman stopped her churning and carefully studied Theodora's serious face. Returning her look, Theodora was amazed by the kindness that sparkled in the wise, hazel eyes.

"Why do you ask, child?" The old woman spoke very, very gently.

"Because I want to love the King. But I can't love him because I don't know him. And if I'm ever going to know him, I've got to find other people who will tell me how to meet him." Her words spilled over each other like the Seabound River cascading along its way. Just then, the sun went behind a cloud, and shadows hid the woman's face—all but her shining eyes.

"Why do you want to love him?"

"Because it's the law of the land," Theodora replied in frustration. Didn't she understand?

"How will you love him, child?"

"How will I love him? How will I love him? I don't know, and I really wish I did. Can't you tell me what to do?"

Just then, the sun reappeared as several clouds
fleeted past, prodded along by the wind. The old woman
was churning again. And as her arms moved, Theodora
caught a glimpse of gold on her bony wrist.

She stared at the gold. It seemed absurdly out of
place against the rough, drab dress. It glimmered and
gleamed in the late afternoon light.

The old lady smiled at Theodora and stopped her
work once again. "Would you like to see my bracelet,
child?"

She didn't remove it. It seemed too much a part of
her arm ever to come off. As Theodora looked closely,
she could see five words carved in simple letters on the
radiant metal: *To Love Is to Serve.*

"Where did you get it?" Theodora whispered, shivering with delight. Suddenly, she remembered the blazing,
emerald eye the workman wore around his neck. The
woman laughed, and her laughter rang out like a young
girl's. "Oh," she smiled, with a wave of her hand, "I've
had it for years."

"What does it mean, *to love is to serve?* What does
that mean?"

"There is a legend in our village, and I learned it as a
girl, small as you, child. Within the legend is the mean-
ing of the words *to love is to serve.*"

"Tell me! Tell me the legend!" Theodora cried.
"Please!" she added, hoping not to sound impolite.

"It's really very simple, child. The legend says only
this: The King wears many faces—old faces and young,
rich faces and poor, strange faces and familiar, plain
faces and beautiful. And the very person you serve may
be the King himself!"

Theodora's first thought was one of joy. The legend gave her hope and a feeling that she was on the right path toward knowing the King.

Her second thought, however, plunged her into sadness. She thought of her hard-working mother, of her little sisters who had tried to help her, and of her older sisters who had felt the brunt of her rude words earlier that day. She swallowed hard, looked up at the old lady, and sighed, "So that's how I can love the King. If I'd just help someone else . . ."

The old woman hadn't seemed to hear Theodora at all. With a faraway look in her eyes, she continued to speak. "There's a little song we used to sing as children . . ." And in a voice that sounded like dry autumn leaves, she began an odd, sing-song tune.

> Milk to pour and words to keep,
> Flowers to pick and floors to sweep,
> Never mind for whom it's done,
> The King could be most anyone.
> Flocks to tend and cows to feed,
> Wood to chop and fields to seed,
> Kindly do most anything,
> And you'll have done it for the King.

When she finished the song, the old, brown woman seemed to forget that Theodora was even there. She churned and churned and never replied at all when Theodora said goodbye. By the time Theodora looked back from across the little pasture, the old lady had vanished into the shadows of the workshed.

Milk to pour and words to keep, Flowers to pick and . . . Theodora absently sang the little song to herself, thinking and dreaming and wondering. All at once, she stopped abruptly. Five unfamiliar children—three boys and two girls—suddenly appeared out of nowhere. She started to greet them cheerfully, but the sight of their unfriendly, sallow faces made the word *hello* vanish from her lips.

Angry eyes scowled at Theodora, and smirking expressions curved the corners of the strangers' mouths most unpleasantly. Then one of the children began to sing in a mocking tone, "Milk to pour and words to keep, Flowers to pick and floors to sweep, Never mind for whom it's done . . ."

The others chimed in, their voices surly and spiteful, every word growing louder and more scornful. They joined hands and made a ring around Theodora.

Theodora felt frightened—very frightened, to be sure. She had never before seen any of these hard-faced children, and she had thought she knew every child in Place. These children seemed somehow dangerous, and she would have to run a good distance to reach the safety of her home.

An uneasy question stirred within her. How did these children know the words to the song? Had they been hiding and listening as she and the old woman had talked?

Just then she remembered the workman's warning, "Watch out for the Children of the South. . . ."

That's who they are. I know it. Theodora shivered as she looked at their sneering faces. What would they do to her? Why were they so angry? How would she ever get home?

FOUR

A BOY FROM THE CITY OF BELLS

Young Arlen had hair the color of pale wheat and eyes as blue as the sapphire sky around the castle. He sat beside a lace-curtained window in his grandmother's house and stared out into the fading afternoon light. It was late in the afternoon on his first day at Place-Beneath-the-Castle, and the past twelve hours had been long and lonely.

Arlen watched sunset-stained clouds scudding across the sky and wondered if his parents could see them from their home in the City of Bells. He felt so far away from them, and deep in his heart, he knew very well that they wouldn't miss him at all.

He had made the long journey from the city in a beautiful, horse-drawn carriage just the day before. His father's livery man, Charles, had carefully packed Arlen's bags and driven the boy himself to Granma's house in Place-Beneath-the-Castle.

"You're a good boy, son," The faithful servant had told the blonde boy, ruffling his hair with a calloused hand. "I think you'll have a happier time with your grandmother, and I know she'll take good care of you."

At that moment, Granma had come bustling out of her little cottage. In spite of his heavy heart, Arlen had smiled when he'd seen her, round and rosy and crowned with a coronet of gold-gray hair. "Arlen, my sweet boy, welcome to my home! It's far smaller than what you're used to, I know. But you'll soon feel as if you've lived here all your life!"

Small Arlen had thrown his arms around Granma's waist and wept uncontrollably. Charles had shaken his head sadly. Waving a silent farewell, the livery man had driven off without another word.

Granma had taken the boy into a warm cottage, fragrant with the smell of newly baked cookies, and had shown him a ladder that led up to a tiny loft. There he had found a quilt-covered bed with a soft white pillow, a small wooden table, and a simple chair beside the window where he now sat. It was a cozy room, brightened by a bouquet of freshly picked roses. In spite of his homesickness, Arlen was ever so glad to be here.

I've heard that people have seen the King's castle from here, Arlen thought to himself. *I'm going to see it, too. I know there's a King, and I'm going to meet him someday, no matter what my father says.*

Arlen's father was a stern man, with gray eyes as cold as granite. He was well known in the City of Bells for his wealth. He was better known for his cruelty.

Arlen's mother was a beauty, to be sure. But she rarely smiled and never spoke to her only son except to correct him. That was more attention than Arlen received from his father, however.

His father never spoke to him at all.

Arlen had every toy that had ever been made. He had a pony and a painted boat in a lagoon and a stern nurse, who taught the bright boy his lessons with a strict and steadfast hand. The only thing Arlen lacked was love. Yet, even though he'd never really experienced love except on Granma's rare visits, he believed with all his heart that it was important. And, perhaps because of his grandmother, his child's heart had always sensed that love had something to do with the mysterious King who lived in those far off, treacherous mountains.

Arlen had heard his father bellow with rage at the very mention of the King. His mother had sneered and cursed when he had asked her about the castle. Nurse had stung his hand soundly with a switch when the question had come up during history lessons.

But Granma, during her rare visits to her wealthy son and daughter-in-law in the City of Bells, had answered his questions far differently. She had reached over and touched her grandson's face softly. "You'll see, Arlen. You'll see."

"When, Granma? When will I see?"

"When you come and live with me next year."

"I'm coming to live with you?" Some unfamiliar new hope fluttered in the boy's heart.

"Your parents are very busy people, Arlen. But as for me, I have nothing more important to do than care for my only grandson. I'll make you cookies, take you walking, and show you the King's castle when the clouds clear away." Granma, well aware that Arlen's tyrannical father would have no kind words for her if he should overhear, had lowered her voice when she had mentioned the King.

So here Arlen was at last, gazing out his new window toward the towering pinnacles of the mountains, straining his eyes to see if the castle just might appear in the sunset sky.

I'll go out and take a look around. Maybe I'll be able to see it better from somewhere in the fields.

"Granma, do you mind if I go for a walk?"

"Of course not, Arlen. Just be back before dark."

A single star pierced the twilight sky as he wandered down Granma's path, past her gardens, and toward the pastures beyond. The boy fixed his eyes on the mountains. Was that a glimmer of silver he saw at the very top of the highest peak? Was it a rising star? Or was it a turret on the King's castle?

He squinted into the fading light, focusing all his attention on the horizon. Then he heard a strange noise. It sounded like children singing, but there was something dreadfully unpleasant about their song. "Milk to pour and words to keep, Flowers to pick and floors to sweep . . ."

Arlen turned his eyes from the mountains and toward the singing. He saw six children. Five had formed a ring around a brown-haired girl who sat on her knees on the ground, her face in her hands, looking very frightened, indeed.

Arlen recognized the hateful sound of the children's harsh, angry voices. He had heard that sound often among the many children in the City of Bells. Arlen began to run toward the boys and girls. Once he reached them, he immediately realized that the five chil-

Five children had formed a ring around a brown-haired girl.

dren in the ring were tormenting the little girl in the
center.

"Get away from her!" he shouted, using his father's
harshest tones. The authority in his voice surprised even
him, and his unexpected approach caused the five children to scatter, running from the golden-haired boy.
Fear flashed in their scowling eyes.

"Who are you?" Theodora arose from her knees,
brushed away the dirt, and wiped her eyes on her
sleeve. She repeated the question. "Who are you? Did
you come from the King?"

"The King? Do you know the King?" Arlen's face
glowed with wonder as he looked at the calico-dressed
girl with the wide, gentle eyes.

"No, I don't know him yet. But I've spent most of
the day looking for people who do, and I thought you
might be another friend of his. Your hair is so golden,
you *look* like a King's messenger. Well, at least *I* think
you do!"

Arlen beamed with delight at Theodora's words.
Then he remembered his manners just in time to introduce himself. "My name is Arlen, and I've come to live
in Place-Beneath-the-Castle with my grandmother.
What's your name?"

"My name is Theodora. Do you know those other
children? I was so afraid of them. Thank you for chasing
them away!"

"I don't know them, but I know others who are very
much like them. There are many such children in the
City of Bells, on the south side. They serve the Six Cruel
Kings. I think my own father may have some dealing

with those kings. He is not known for his kindness, either. Believe me."

Theodora shivered at the way Arlen's voice hardened when he mentioned his father. "My father is a good man," she said softly. "Would you like to meet him?"

Arlen couldn't imagine a father he would ever want to know. "Some other time, Theodora. But tell me about the King. *That's* who I want to meet. And I will someday. I *will* meet him, no matter what."

"Oh, I hope you do! For me, it's not so much that I want to meet him. But I really want to love him, and I think I'll have to meet him if I'm ever going to love him."

"Why do you want to love him?"

"Because it's the law of the land. I don't want to break the law."

Theodora's eyes were so wide and sincere, her words so open and genuine, that Arlen almost felt like weeping. His feelings about the King were far different from hers. He secretly wanted to meet someone with more authority than his father—someone who would stop the brutal man's merciless acts, someone who would teach him about justice, someone who would force him to take notice of his son.

"Well, Theodora, we're looking for the same King, aren't we? And I think we need to work together, don't you?"

"Maybe so," Theodora answered, her brown eyes soft with dreams. "Maybe you're one of the King's children, too. That's what the workman told me I am. A child of the King. Isn't that a wonderful thought?"

"Yes, of course. Wonderful. Now tell me, Theodora, have you seen the castle? I thought I saw a glint of silver

just awhile ago, from Granma's house. Could that have
been it?"

"Of course it was, Arlen! It was. Sometimes it looks
like a bank of clouds, sometimes like a sapphire gleam in
the morning, and often at twilight it looks like a silver
shimmer, just below the evening star." Her voice grew
tender as she spoke about the castle.

Arlen looked at Theodora, joy sparkling in his blue
eyes. "You're just the person I needed to meet. Will you
tell me everything you know? I promise not to tell another soul—not even Granma. Will you tell me?"

Theodora considered his request for a moment.
Then she remembered, *to love is to serve.* Wouldn't it
be a sort of service to tell Arlen everything she knew
about the King?

And so she described to Arlen the young lovers and
how they had instructed her to love the King with her
heart. She explained to him about the minstrel and
about loving the King with her soul. She informed him
about the wise woman from the City of Bells who had
charged her that she must love the King with her mind.
She told Arlen about the workman with the emerald eye
and about the old woman with the bracelet of gold. All
those tales poured from her young, eager lips like waters
from a sweet mountain spring. But then she stopped.

What about the rainbow messenger? She paused for
nearly a half a minute.

"What's wrong, Theodora?" Arlen looked at his new
friend with concern in his eyes. "Is there something else?"

"I'm afraid to tell you the rest. I'm afraid you'll think
I imagined it, or that I'm lying, or that . . ."

"Why don't you let me decide for myself?"

But somehow, the words couldn't find their way out of Theodora's mouth just then. She looked into Arlen's intelligent young face and wanted very much to be his friend. But the rainbow messenger was something she held dear to her heart. It would have to wait until she knew the boy better.

"I'll tell you later, I promise. Anyway, you've got plenty to think about, don't you, Arlen? And tomorrow, if you like, we can continue our search together. Why don't you meet me at the crossroads in the apple grove? We'll go from there."

Not wanting to seem ignorant, Arlen nodded his head. *Granma will know where the crossroads is,* he assured himself. "I'll see you there mid-morning, then."

"Thanks again for frightening off those unkind children, Arlen. I don't know what might have happened if you hadn't."

"Neither do I. In fact, why don't I walk home with you," he suggested, suddenly feeling very strong and brave, "just in case they show up again?"

Arlen and Theodora strolled across the fields together, while one star after another appeared in the deep blue sky. Far off in the distance, a castle of purest silver shone in full glory atop a high, craggy pinnacle.

"You see?" Theodora pointed toward the mountains.

"I see. I knew it all along." Arlen, awed by the reality of seeing a dream come true, spoke in a whisper.

"It's nice to have a friend who's looking for the same thing I am." Theodora smiled at Arlen as they said goodbye.

"It's nice to have a friend at all," Arlen answered quite gravely, thinking of his lonely house in the City of Bells.

"Are you sure you don't want to meet my mother and father?"

"Not now. Some other day. I'll see you tomorrow, Theodora."

With that, Arlen turned and ran across the fields toward Granma's little cottage. He felt as if he had wings on his feet, such happiness surged inside him. Imagine really having seen the castle! And imagine having a friend who was just as interested in the King as he was!

As for Theodora, her own joy was short lived. Her father caught her by the arm and stopped her as she rushed through the door of the cottage. His face was drawn, gray with fear.

"Shhhh, child. Walk softly."

"Father, what is it? Whatever is wrong?"

"It's your mother, Theodora. She's not supposed to be having the new baby yet, but it's coming anyway."

"Isn't it good if it comes early?"

"No, it isn't good at all, little one. The baby could die, and so could Mother."

Without a thought about supper or another word, Theodora went to her little bed. She noticed her sisters, silent in the evening light, were lying in their own beds. Shaking with fear at the thought of losing Mother, she pulled on her long, white nightgown and crawled under her quilt. She thought of the King and of her search for him. She had not been kind to her mother because of it. How foolish it all seemed at this terrible moment. And yet . . .

"Oh, King," she whispered, "the rainbow messenger said that you feel and know and understand. Do you feel as bad as I do about my mother and the new baby? Do you know what to do? Do you understand how awful it would be if . . ."

Theodora couldn't say another word. She stuffed her pillow in her mouth so no one could hear her. And, trembling in the darkness, she cried herself to sleep.

FIVE

MIDNIGHT MESSENGERS

hen Theodora awoke, it was still completely dark outside. A candle burning in her mother's bedroom cast a golden light around the corner into the room she shared with three of her sisters. She rubbed her eyes and remembered the reason they felt so swollen and sore. She had been weeping, afraid that her mother might die.

Was she still alive?

Theodora threw back her blankets and quietly climbed out of bed. Tiptoeing carefully on her way to check on Mother, she suddenly heard the sound that had awakened her—a muffled tap, tap, tap at the front door. Had anyone else heard it?

She grabbed the quilt from her bed, wrapped it around her shoulders, and opened the door. There stood a middle-aged gentleman with a kind face and concern in his eyes.

"Your mother is ill," he whispered. "I've come to help."

Letting him inside the door, Theodora ran into her parents' room. Her father sat in a chair at Mother's side, staring into the darkness. "Father! A man is here to help!"

43

"What man?" He rose stiffly to his feet and walked to the door, where the man waited just inside.

"Sir?" Theodora's father spoke to the man a bit harshly. "How did you know my wife was ill?"

The man shook his head and shrugged his shoulders. "I was sent by a friend, and I've come to help." Reaching inside his coat, he pulled out a small, blue bottle capped with a silvery lid. "This medicine will save her and the infant as well. Put a little in a spoon, and place it inside her mouth. She will soon improve."

His mission complete, the middle-aged man bowed slightly, turned, and left the house. Outside, Theodora could see a blanket of stars across the sky but not even the thread of a new moon. In the distance, the castle was in full view, and somehow it seemed closer than ever before. She turned, wanting to point it out to Father, but he had already disappeared inside the house.

The King . . . she thought to herself. *The medicine is from the King.*

"Father, I'll get the spoon." She rushed into the kitchen, which was completely shrouded in darkness, and felt around in a cupboard until her hand touched the cutlery. She grasped a spoon, hurried into the bedroom, and handed it to her father, who stood weeping beside his wife's bed.

"It may be too late, child." He stared at Theodora's mother, who lay pale and motionless, the flickering candle creating eerie shadows upon her face.

"It can't be too late. The King would never be too late. . . ."

"What's this got to do with the King?" There was anger in his voice, and he snatched the spoon from his

daughter's shaky hand. "I'd like to know who that man
was and who told him she's sick. I don't like strangers
coming in the middle of the night, no matter how good
their intentions. If she weren't so . . . so sick, I wouldn't
even try this."

Theodora didn't dare to say another word. For the
first time in her life, she was almost afraid her father
might strike her. He was trembling, too, and he spilled a
little of the bottle's clear liquid as he measured out a single spoonful, placed it gently between his wife's white
lips, and tipped its contents into her mouth.

Father and daughter then stood, silent and expec-
tantly, for several minutes. At first, it seemed that nothing was happening. But then Mother's cheeks began to
regain their lost color. And her eyelids fluttered just a little, as if she might be waking.

And sure enough, after less than a quarter hour's
time, her brown eyes were open, and she was whisper-
ing something to her husband.

The weary man lowered his head to hear her almost
inaudible words. "What is it, love?"

"The baby. It's moving. It's alive, and unless I'm
dreaming, so am I."

Theodora watched the scene in wonder. She reached
over and squeezed her mother's hand and patted the
small mound under the blankets where the baby was.
"Good night, Mother; and good night, little baby. I'll see
you soon!"

She bounded out of the room and leapt back into
her own bed, where she thought and she dreamed and
she wondered. Before much time had passed, she had
fallen into a dreamless sleep.

*a *a *a

The blanket of stars glistened overhead, and the castle gleamed in silver majesty atop the mountains. Arlen awoke suddenly in his tiny loft. What had awakened him? He got up, glanced out the window, and caught his breath. The castle! It was so clear and so perfectly defined that the boy was about to run and wake Granma to share the sight with her.

But right then, as Arlen glanced back at his bed, he realized that someone, or something, was sitting on it! It looked more like a wisp of vapor at first, like a fog composed of every color in the rainbow. But the closer Arlen looked, the more he realized that the shining, shimmering image had a face with eyes, a nose, and a mouth. And then, he heard a voice which reminded him of a cascading river or a mountain waterfall.

"Arlen, I have come to tell you about the King. It is good that you have seen the castle, son. But you have much more to see than that. I've just been to visit your new friend Theodora, and I have brought life back to her mother.

"But I must warn you, grave difficulties will soon come to that family. A mistake will become a mystery, and a mystery will become a marvel, and a marvel will bring new hope to all. In the meantime, however, you must be strong, like a man. And, most important of all, you must think of your friend Theodora more kindly than you think of yourself. These are your instructions from the King.

"And remember, young Arlen, the King feels. The King knows. And the King understands."

The messenger left as quickly as he had appeared.
Arlen sat alone in his room. He felt nearly overcome by
the effort to remember everything that had happened
and the struggle to understand what it meant. His young
mind was bright, but it could not possibly grasp everything all at once. And so, very wisely, he went to his
table, lit a candle, took paper and pen in hand, and
wrote down every word the messenger had said.

Once finished, he whispered softly, "At least I won't
forget anything this way. But I wonder if I should tell
Granma? Or Theodora, for that matter. Would they believe me, or would they think I had imagined the whole
thing?"

Lying in his bed, staring at the ceiling, Arlen was
hard pressed to get back to sleep. So much had happened, and so quickly. What did the being mean, "I
have brought life back to her mother"?

And what mistake would become a mystery, and
what mystery would become a marvel, and what . . .

Round and round his head the thoughts and questions danced until at last Arlen slept, thoroughly exhausted by his efforts to understand.

Come sunrise, a choir of birds awakened the boy,
who stretched and yawned and then hurried to his table
to read the words he'd written in the middle of the
night. *One thing at a time,* he told himself. *First, I'll
make a copy to carry in my pocket, and I'll keep the
other one here—just in case.*

By the time he climbed down the ladder and walked
into the kitchen for breakfast, he had carefully tucked
the second copy of his notes into his breast pocket.
"Good morning, Granma!"

"Good morning, Arlen. Did you sleep well, grandson?"

He looked at Granma's kind, rosy face. *I won't tell her. I will tell Theodora.* "Couldn't have slept better if I'd wanted to. Granma, I've made a new friend named Theodora, and I've promised to meet her at the cross-roads mid-morning. Is it far to the crossroads?"

"Not far at all, Arlen. Once you've helped me with some chores, I'll point you in the right direction, and you'll be there in plenty of time. Now, when you've finished eating, would you feed the chickens for me and be sure they have enough water?"

Three hours later found Arlen running across fields beneath a heavy sky that dropped an occasional splattering raindrop on his face. The clear night had grown cloudy long before dawn. The mountains had vanished from sight, and with them the castle. Arlen, stopping to get his bearings, pulled his collar around his neck to shield himself from the chill. There they were, just ahead—the apple grove and the fork in the road. And there was Theodora, lost in dreams, wrapped in a brown, woolen cape and sitting on her favorite rock. "Oh, Arlen!" She smiled brightly when he appeared. "I was afraid you'd forgotten!"

"No, I wasn't likely to forget. But something happened that makes our meeting even more important than I'd ever imagined. Take a look at this."

Just as he pulled the carefully folded, neatly printed notes out of his pocket, a huge clap of thunder crashed nearby, and the boy and girl ran to find shelter in an old shed standing in a nearby field.

It was dark inside the shed, and it was hard for Theodora to see the words, but at last, with Arlen's help, she was able to read what he had written. "But it makes no sense, Arlen. Is it a poem or some sort of a riddle?"

"Theodora, I'm afraid you aren't going to believe what I'm about to tell you." He stopped short, interrupted by another flash of lightning and the roar of thunder that followed. By now, drenching rain was pouring out of the sky, soaking the soil and bending the trees.

Theodora looked at the solemn expression on her new friend's face and remembered how she'd felt the night before, when she'd started to tell him about the rainbow messenger.

"If it has to do with the King, I'll believe anything you tell me. I have a story of my own to tell you, once you've told me yours."

Arlen tried to describe the rainbow messenger, but words failed him. Theodora quickly understood.

"Was he made up of all sorts of colors?"

Arlen nodded mutely.

"And could you sort of see through him?"

He nodded again.

"And did his voice sound like a waterfall?"

"That's him! You must have seen him, too. He came to your house last night, didn't he?"

"Someone did. Someone brought medicine to Mother, and no one knew she was sick, except . . ."

"Except what, Theodora?"

"Except . . . Oh, Arlen, you see, I told the King."

"How on earth did you tell the King?" He looked at the girl in astonishment, afraid to imagine what might happen next.

"I just whispered into the darkness because, you see, the rainbow messenger I saw a long time ago told me that the King feels, and he knows, and he understands. . . ."

"And so the King heard you. He sent the messenger to help your mother, and then he came by my house on his way back to the castle."

"He wasn't a rainbow messenger when he came to my house. He was just a man. But wait! That's just what the workman said! The messenger who gave him the emerald eye appeared first as an ordinary person and then later as a rainbow messenger."

"It must have been the same person." Arlen and Theodora looked at each other very, very soberly. "The King wants us to be friends, doesn't he?"

"Yes, Theodora, but more than that, he wants to prepare us for something that's coming—something to do with your family. Look."

Grave difficulties will soon come to that family. A mistake will become a mystery. A mystery will become a marvel. A marvel will bring new hope to all. But meanwhile, you must think of your friend Theodora more kindly than you think of yourself.

Theodora shivered. "I hope it's nothing to do with Mother and the new baby. Will you come back to my house with me, just long enough to make sure she's all right?"

Through puddles and showers and patches of sunshine, the boy and girl ran all the way to Theodora's cottage. When they arrived, they found the girl's mother in the kitchen, singing and sweeping the floor.

"Mother, you should be in bed!" Theodora cried, snatching the broom out of her hands and beginning to sweep.

"I'm fine, child. I am perfectly fine. But I can't understand who the man was who came to the door. Is he a friend of yours?"

"No, Mother, but this is my friend Arlen. He's new in Place, and he's going to be a good friend to all of us."

"I'm pleased to meet you, son. Why don't you and Theodora have the last two pieces of this pie before you go?" She pulled what was left of a homemade berry cobbler out of the pantry and cut it in half.

They shared the pie and drank mugs of milk. Just before they ran outside to pursue their search, Theodora went into her parent's room and picked up the small, blue bottle that sat on the bedside table.

"Have you ever seen such silver as the cap on that bottle?" The girl's mother shook her head at the sight of it. "It's so shiny, it looks almost alive."

"It looks like the castle in the moonlight, ma'am." Arlen offered softly.

Theodora's mother laughed merrily. She hugged her daughter fondly against her side and softly touched Arlen's cheek. "I can see that you and Theodora have much in common. Kings and castles and magic bottles should give you plenty to dream about for the rest of the summer!"

SIX

SINGERS
AND SIX KINGS

ost in melancholy thoughts, their chins firmly
planted in their hands, Theodora and Arlen had
nary a word to say to each other. It had been a dis-
mal and disappointing morning, and the events of early afternoon had not improved their humor in the least.

The two had begun their day with the best possible intentions. They had decided to find the workman with the
emerald eye and then to go see the old woman with the
gold bracelet. Theodora had meant to introduce Arlen to
each of them, so he could hear their stories for himself.

Once those visits had been accomplished, they would
sit in the apple grove at the crossroads, watching for the lovers or the minstrel or the wise woman. Perhaps one of
them would tell Theodora even more about loving the
King. Afterwards, Arlen could ask them his own questions.

But alas, not one thing had happened as they had
planned. They had searched every stone-fenced field
and looked beneath every last tree on the Cloudwarren
farm, but the green-eyed workman was nowhere to be
found. And when Theodora had politely inquired at the
farmhouse as to his whereabouts, the housewife had replied tartly, "I've got no idea what you're talking about,

53

child. Must be some stranger my husband hired without telling me. He does that, y' know." She'd sniffed, scowled, and closed the door quite firmly in Theodora's face.

Then, on the heels of that failure, the whitewashed shed in which Theodora had first met the old woman had turned up altogether empty—no trace of a churn, or even a cow, in sight.

So now the two children, nursing private doubts and secret suspicions, sat in the apple grove. Arlen looked at Theodora out of the corner of his blue eye. There she was, all innocence and honesty. Maybe she'd made up the whole story of the workman, and maybe the old woman had been a figment of her very active imagination.

Theodora was a nice enough girl, to be sure. And yes, he'd seen the castle and the rainbow messenger, too. But maybe, just maybe, Theodora didn't know what was true from what wasn't. Maybe she was an exaggerator. Maybe she was even a liar!

And, as if in response to her friend's silent accusations, Theodora took a sidelong glance at Arlen and began to consider her own uncertainties about him. If he really was a child of the King, why had everything become so difficult since his arrival in Place? The handsome boy had certainly shown up at the right time, saving her from the unkind children. But maybe there was more to him than met the eye. Maybe Arlen was one of the evil children himself! Maybe he had come along to lead her away from the King instead of to help her find him!

To the children's credit, neither of them said a word about their ugly, unfair thoughts. They both felt almost as miserable and gloomy inside as the day itself.

For oh, what a dreary day it was! The sky was gray and motionless as stone. Not a breeze stirred, not a bird caroled, not a bee buzzed. The castle was nowhere to be seen, for the mountains had vanished into the overcast sky. An unusual quiet seemed to have cloaked the countryside in foreboding. Both children shivered, even though the air wasn't especially cold.

And then, the choir appeared.

Later on, neither Arlen nor Theodora could remember who had heard the singing first. At the beginning, it had sounded like cowbells tinkling in some distant pasture. But as it had drawn closer, they had realized it was clearly a song with words and a tune. Lovely voices had sent it drifting across the land.

> We are free from the worry, we are free
>   from the pain,
> We are warm, though we journey through the night
>   and the rain.
> Great the King who has brought us from the dead,
>   for we live!
> Great the King who has taught us—Those who love
>   must forgive!

Arlen and Theodora lifted their heads and exclaimed at the same time, "Listen!" And then they jumped up and scanned the roadways, searching for the singers of the beautiful song.

They looked behind them, toward Castle Street, but no one was there. They peered down from the crossroads in the direction of the City of Bells, but the highway was empty. Then they lifted their eyes toward the mountains, down the narrow lane that led into the foothills. There they saw them—thirty or more men and women, boys and girls.

Every one of them was dressed in pale shades of blue and violet. The girls wore garlands of flowers in their hair. The boys had their arms full of blossoms. The men and women carried silver banners on which a single word was exquisitely stitched: *Love.*

Smiling faces surrounded Theodora and Arlen before they even realized what was happening, and warm arms embraced them. The people who greeted them seemed to feel they'd known Theodora and Arlen all their lives.

"Two children of the King, if I've ever seen them!"

"Children of the King, to be sure!"

Everyone seemed to be saying things like that, and both children were nearly overwhelmed by all the happy greetings.

"Your song is beautiful," Theodora told one of the children shyly. "What does it mean, something about being brought from the dead?"

"We were all dead, and the King gave us back our lives again!"

Arlen cringed a little, but he tried to sound brave as he asked, "Are you ghosts, then?"

Everyone laughed uproariously at his polite inquiry. "Of course we're not ghosts! In fact, considering what's happened, we're probably more alive than you are!" One of the older men tousled Arlen's hair affectionately as he answered.

Arlen wanted more information. "How could the King bring you back from the dead?"

"He has the power because he was once dead himself."

"What?" Theodora refused to believe the King was ever dead. "He couldn't have been dead! How did he die?"

"Many years ago, the Six Cruel Kings and their followers stormed the castle and murdered him. Little did they know how strong his love would be! He had so much love in his heart that he came back to life. And ever since, he's given life back to all the people who die, *if* they believe he's really there in the castle. Usually they stay there with him, but he's sent us back to the kingdom."

One of the men, who had a very earnest face, added, "Of course, the Six Cruel Kings keep lying about the King, saying that he's still dead."

"We *know* he's in the castle!" shouted Arlen and Theodora at almost exactly the same time.

"We knew he was there, too, even before we saw him," said a black-haired little boy with eyes as deep as midnight. "You see, every one of us died because someone killed us, either accidently or on purpose. The King gave us back our lives, but the first thing he asked us to do was to forgive the people who killed us."

A teenage girl interrupted, "That's right, and then he sent us back to the kingdom to tell the people here to forgive each other."

Theodora was puzzled. "Forgive each other for what?"

"For anything they've ever done to hurt each other."

"That's easy," said Theodora, who had precious little to forgive in her young life.

"That's impossible," muttered Arlen, who had grown noticeably stiff and stern during the excited conversation.

"You, son," a kindly woman said, lowering her flag as she hugged a reluctant Arlen, "have much adventure ahead of you. And forgiveness lies at the end of your journey, just as it lay at the end of ours."

"Before you go . . ." Theodora felt a burst of panic, noticing that some of the grownups were beginning to line up again. "Wait! What is the King like? Tell me about the King!"

"The King is the most wonderful, joyful person I've ever seen," answered a brown-haired woman, turning to go.

Then several of the children answered Theodora's question, and it seemed as if they were all talking at once.

"The King is young, but he is wise like an old man."

"The King has the happiest laugh, but his eyes are very serious when he speaks to you."

"The King acts like he's known you all your life, *and* he makes you feel like he really enjoys being with you."

Finally, a tiny boy stepped forward, his face round as the full moon, a halo of golden curls on his head. "The King is love," he lisped. "If you want to know what love feels like, just sit on the lap of the King."

At that moment, the choir began to move toward Castle Street, singing as they went. Their lovely melody drifted across the fields toward the two children, faded once again into the sound of tinkling cowbells, and finally could be heard no more.

"Arlen, wasn't that glorious!" Theodora was all but dancing in circles around her friend. "I know I'm going to love the King, maybe even before I ever see him! Doesn't he sound like someone you could love?"

"I will never forgive my father." The boy's voice was icy, and his blue eyes looked gray as granite in the late afternoon light.

"Whatever has he done to you?" Theodora felt as if someone had poured a bucket of snow over her warm heart. Arlen looked so angry, so bitter. Yet in spite of herself, she wanted to understand.

"I am his son, and he refuses to love me. I don't want to forgive him or to love him or anything else. I want the King to punish him for the way he has treated me all my life. I hate my father, and I will never forgive him."

A chill rippled up and down Theodora's back at the sound of Arlen's words. With nothing more to say, the boy and girl headed toward their homes. But just before they parted, Theodora took Arlen's hand in hers and kissed his cheek. "The King will help you," she said. "He feels. And he knows. And he understands."

In that unexpected moment of friendship, neither Arlen nor Theodora heard the sound of rustling feet in the woods nearby. They didn't see the darting, furtive eyes that watched them. They didn't hear the whispered orders, "Run to the courier! Give him the report!"

❧ ❧ ❧

Hours later, in the City of Bells, a strange scene took place. In a dark, smoky grotto beneath the city streets, five old men sat in throne-like chairs around a marble table. A sixth chair remained empty. Each man had a craggy, scowling face with eyes as black as death. Each wore a robe the color of a gemstone. Each white head was crowned with a circlet of ebony. Ten hands were folded on the table like tangled birds' claws.

Just then the sixth old man entered the room, roughly dragging a younger nobleman along by the arm.

"Let go of me!" the nobleman snarled at the old man, trying to jerk himself free of his bony grasp. "I said, let me go!"

At those words, all five of the men around the table
rose to their feet. In a voice cold as steel, the eldest of
them spoke, his eyes glittering with malice above his gar-
net robe. "You will not speak to any of us in that way,
fool. Either you will address us with respect, or you will
never speak again."

A thud echoed through the room as the older man
threw the young nobleman down onto the floor. The old
man's face, red with rage, looked even ruddier in the
light of the torches that flamed from the rock walls.

The nobleman rose to his feet with as much dignity
as he could muster. He brushed off his elegant clothing,
adjusted his satin jacket, and glared into the six pairs of
evil eyes that glared back at him.

"Dear sirs, forgive my annoyance." His voice dripped
with sarcasm. "I have served the six of you well for many
years. I have sacrificed for you and have encouraged
many others to join your service as well. How could I
possibly deserve such ill treatment?"

The old man who had brought him into the room
shoved him down again, kicked him, then glowered over
him like a vulture. "You have done much for our cause,
indeed. But you have overlooked one rather important
matter."

"And what might that be?"

"Your son, Arlen, you detestable fool. He is seeking
information about our enemy and has even expressed a
determination to know him. He is a dangerous boy, and
he has a new friend even more dangerous than he is."

"What kind of a friend?"

*The sixth old man entered the room, roughly dragging
a younger nobleman along by the arm.*

"A little girl."

"What are you talking about?" The man laughed rudely and loudly. "Out of line as they are, these two are children—nothing but babes! How can you be so concerned about the fantasies of children?"

The old man slapped him.

"You absolute idiot! Don't you know that children are the enemy's most valuable servants? They do more to promote the lie of his existence than all the adults in the kingdom put together."

"What do you mean, the lie of his existence! You know very well that he's alive, and so do I!"

The bony man struck a painful blow across Arlen's father's face. His lower lip began to bleed, and he was momentarily stunned.

"No one cares what you think or know. Listen and beware! The enemy is dispatching his wretched messengers throughout the kingdom in ever-increasing numbers. He has sent a troupe of actors out, pretending they have been raised from the dead. And he is courting children like your arrogant son to do his foul bidding.

"Therefore, we are commanding you to stop your boy from his inquiries and to silence his little friend. Stop them immediately, or you will not live to see another winter."

Humbled by the harsh blow to his chin and frightened by the threat, Arlen's father stood up, steadied himself, and then spoke quietly and firmly.

"I will go to Place tomorrow, your majesties. I will obey your orders. And when I am finished, mark my words: neither my disgusting son, Arlen, nor his little girlfriend will wish to hear about or know about or even *think* about the Ki . . . the enemy—ever again!"

SEVEN

AN
UNWELCOME
VISITOR

Rain fell in torrents, moving across the countryside like gray curtains in the wind, brushing
wetly across grasses and leaves as it went. Arlen
sat in his loft, writing down everything he could remember about the pastel-clad choir and their words about
the King.

By now he had grown used to their song of forgiveness. Although he had no intention of forgiving his father, he agreed, in principle, to the fact that other people should be forgiven for lesser offenses. He added
today's notes to the earlier ones about the rainbow messenger and included a description of some incidents
along the way. He wanted to be sure he didn't forget
anything, just in case he needed to remember the words
on some future occasion.

It was so dark and gloomy that Arlen was writing by
candlelight. Rain roared against the roof of the cottage,
and beads of moisture hung from the rafters. Gusts of
wind blew through cracks in the walls, flickering the candlelight as he wrote. He was concentrating very hard on

his efforts and had just about finished with his second copy of notes when he heard the sound of a horse's hooves outside.

Arlen was curious to see who might be traveling on such a stormy day, but he did not want to tear himself away from his work. Instead, he waited until he heard a knock on the door. What a sickening ripple of fear he felt when he recognized his father's voice!

"Hello, Mother," the man said, trying to sound friendly.

"Son! What a wonderful surprise! Have you come to see Arlen? He'll be so pleased! Would you like a cup of tea?"

"Yes, of course I would. I'm soaked to the skin."

Arlen listened to the sound of mother and son talking in the kitchen, and his anger swelled with every word.

Father is up to something. He would never have come here except to cause trouble. I wish Granma would quit talking to him about me.

". . . and he's made friends with the most delightful child named Theodora."

"What is she like? Does she come from a large family?"

"Oh, yes, Greyton. It's large, and a very close family as well. They seem to be such lovely people, and the children all adore their mother and father, which is so nice to see."

"What kind of work does the father do?"

"He has a small farm, and his sons help him with it. They have very little money, but they always seem to keep food on the table."

"What is the father's name?"

"Brighton, I believe, is the family name. His first name is Burke. They live on the next farm east."

"Burke Brighton, eh?" There was a conniving tone to the man's voice that made his son feel like screaming.

He's up to no good, Granma. Listen to the questions he's asking! Why would he want to know all that!

"Where's Arlen? I need to have a word with him."

"Oh, he's upstairs in his room—your old room, dear. I'll go get him."

Arlen heard Granma rustling through the house, and soon he saw her rosy, beaming face at the top of the ladder. "Arlen!" she whispered excitedly. "Guess who's here to see you? Your father has come! You see, he *does* love you!"

Arlen looked at her in disbelief. Surely she didn't think that was true. How could she be so blind to her son's ways?

"I'll be right down. Thanks, Granma."

Arlen carefully hid all his notes under his mattress before he went down the ladder. His father, fidgeting nervously with the handle of his teacup, sat glowering at the table.

Up to no good! I just know it!

Greyton Ardourman was a proud man, and he had no concept of his only son's immense hatred for him. He fancied instead that Arlen longed for his company and would very much want to please him in order to gain his favor. He underestimated the boy's intelligence and wrongly assumed that Arlen was afraid of him.

"Arlen! How are you, boy? Listen, I have to talk to you about something very urgent. Mother, would you leave us alone for a moment or two?"

"Of course, dear. Here's a fresh pot of tea. Just help yourselves, won't you?" Granma bustled off, glad to see her two offspring having such a pleasant chat.

Once she was out of the room, the nobleman lowered his voice. "Arlen, I've been hearing some very disturbing things about you and some friend of yours. I hear that you are out talking about the myth of the King, spreading lies that you've met people who know him, and saying that you intend to meet him. Is that true?" Glaring at the boy, he recalled his humiliation of the night before. A purple bruise still stained his chin, bearing witness to the impact of the sixth king's blow.

"You don't believe there's a King anyway, so what difference does it make to you?"

Enraged by the boy's indirect answer, Greyton grabbed him by the arm.

"Is it true, I said?"

"I want to meet the King, but then I have always wanted to. So what? Who's telling you my business anyway?"

"You are my son, and your business is *my* business. Don't you ever forget that!" The man's voice rasped with rage.

"So what is it you want?"

"I want you to stop this search of yours now, at this moment. I want you to tell this child Theodora, or whatever her name is, that she must stop, too. The entire idea must be removed from your minds *today,* or there will be grave consequences."

"Theodora will never stop searching for the King, no matter what I tell her. She wants to . . . to love him."

Arlen's father hit the table with his fist and swore. "Love him, indeed! If she doesn't stop, she will regret every moment she has spent on this ridiculous idea. She will deeply and dearly regret it."

By now the man had thoroughly lost control of his temper. He rose to his feet and towered menacingly over the boy, who remained seated. "Stop it today, at this moment! And stop the girl! If you don't, I will!"

Greyton stormed out of the house without so much as a farewell to his mother. "Burke Brighton, next farm to the east," he muttered to himself as he left. Soon the thunder of his horse's hooves faded into the rush of the rain. Arlen, horrified, realized that his father was headed toward Theodora's house, not toward the City of Bells.

The boy leapt to his feet, desperately trying to collect his thoughts. He had always believed that his father was somehow linked to the Six Cruel Kings, and he knew that the Children of the South served as their spies. So it was no great surprise that his father had heard about his friendship with Theodora. But what was so important about ending their search for the King?

We must be on the right track! Arlen seized the thought. *We must be on the right track, and it must be important for us to continue. Either that, or he'd never try to stop us!*

"Where's your father, Arlen?"

"He's gone, Granma!"

"Oh, I'm sorry I didn't say goodbye to him. Did you two have a nice visit?"

"Granma, Father told me that he wants me to quit searching for the King. And he wants me to force Theodora to do the same. He rode all the way here in the rain to tell me. What do you think about that?"

The woman paused, a worried look causing her forehead to crease deeply. "It must seem important to him. But how does he know what you're doing? Have you written him a letter?"

Arlen put his hands on Granma's shoulder and kissed her fondly. "Granma, you are a good woman, and I love you very much. But you do not know your son very well. And, in some ways, you don't know me very well, either. I'm going to see Theodora right now, rain or no rain."

Arlen ran out the back of the house, covering his head with a feed sack, which was soon thoroughly soaked. When he arrived at Theodora's cottage, he could see his father talking to Burke Brighton beside the animal shed. The two men shook hands, and Greyton immediately mounted his horse and rode off. This time his destination was the City of Bells.

"Theodora, look!" The boy grabbed her arm and pointed toward his father, just before the horse carried him over a hill and out of sight. "That's my father. He came to warn me against our search for the King! Granma told him your father's name, and he came straight here and talked to him. He's told your father to stop you, I'll bet."

"Arlen, how would your father know what we're doing? He lives nearly half a day away. Besides, you told me he's a very busy man. How would he know?"

"I think the Children of the South have sent word to him. Theodora, I believe my father serves the Six Cruel Kings. I really believe he does."

"What will I do if my father tells me to stop searching for the King? I have never once disobeyed him, and
yet . . ." She knelt by the fireplace and began to cry. "I
would never want to hurt my father."

Arlen, wet through and through, sat down right in front
of the fire, his clothes steaming in the heat of the flames. "I
am surely going to disobey *my* father, Theodora. I have no
choice. If it was important enough for him to come all this
way to stop me, then I must *not* stop!"

Just then, Burke Brighton came into the house. He
smiled and kissed Theodora as if nothing were wrong
and walked into the kitchen with a sprightly step.

"Nan, look at this," the children heard him exclaim.
"A nobleman from the City of Bells just came by and
hired me for a job! He's already paid me, and paid me
well. Look at all this money! It's a small fortune! He said
he would send a letter with the details of the job within
a week's time. Meanwhile, we can buy extra food for
you and the children and get the things we need for our
new baby! What a lucky day!"

"What does he want you to do for him, Burke? What
kind of work?"

"Oh, it sounds simple enough. Just delivering messages to someone he knows. Nothing that I can't find
the time to do, I'm sure."

"Who is he? Is he an honest man?"

"I have no reason to think he's not. And why would
he choose me for a dishonest task? There are plenty of
other men in town who have a taste for that kind of
work. I say its a lucky break, and I'm going to enjoy the
extra money, no matter what *you* think, Nan!"

Arlen stared at Theodora, his face white with fear. She was unable to read his thoughts, but a chill shot through her, and she moved closer to the fire. "What are you thinking? What is wrong with you? You look so frightened!" She whispered softly so her parents wouldn't hear.

"Theodora, I think my father has tricked your father. I think the first part of the rainbow being's message has just happened."

"What do you mean?"

"Don't you remember? 'A mistake will become a mystery. . . . ' Your father has made a terrible mistake in dealing with my father. I know he has, even though he'll never believe me."

"Let's tell him!"

"Let's try."

The two children ran to Burke Brighton, and Theodora tugged at his arm. "Father, Arlen needs to tell you something important."

"What is it, son?"

"Sir, we overheard you talking. The man who gave you the money—was it the man you shook hands with out by the animal shed?"

"It was indeed, boy. But you shouldn't be eavesdropping on your elders, you know!" In a happy mood because of his newfound wealth, he tousled the boy's wet hair.

"That man is not to be trusted, sir."

"Now how would you know that, Arlen? He's from the City of Bells."

"And so am I, sir. I know him far better than I wish I did. He's my father, you see. And he is neither a kind man nor a good one."

"Well, I can see no harm in doing a simple task for him, can you?"

"It depends on what the task might be. If you've already spent part of the money before he tells you what he wants, you'll either have to do the job, or he will have you arrested."

"Well then, I'll do the job!"

"What if it is an evil job, sir? What will you do then?"

Burke Brighton paused, thinking hard. Wealth struggled with reason in his mind, and wealth quickly prevailed.

"Arlen, you have a bitter spirit toward your father. He seems a reasonably good man to me, and besides, he trusted me enough to pay me in advance. I would mind my manners if I were you, boy. And when I need your advice about my business, I'll surely ask. Do you hear?" Burke had always thought Arlen was a bit too smart for his own good.

Arlen and Theodora looked at each other with horror in their eyes. They returned to the fireplace, dejected and depressed. For several moments they didn't speak.

"There's nothing more we can do, Theodora," Arlen murmured eventually, shaking his head sadly. "He's already annoyed with me. And he'll be angry with you, too, if you say another word."

"I guess we'll just have to wait and see what the job turns out to be. Maybe it won't be so bad after all, Arlen. And it would be nice to have extra food on the table, especially for Mother. She's going to have the baby in less than a month, and she needs to be strong!"

The rain had all but ceased when Arlen headed back to his cottage alone. He shoved his cold hands into his pockets and trudged slowly through muddy fields. His insides were boiling with dread.

"Grave difficulties will soon come to that family. A mistake will become a mystery. . . ." So much had happened since the rainbow messenger's visit. What kind of grave difficulties had the being foreseen? And what else had he said?

"You must think of your friend Theodora more kindly than you think of yourself. These are your instructions from the King."

Arlen's heart ached for the girl. She loved her father so dearly, and he could not help but believe that fearful days lay ahead for Burke Brighton.

Sometimes I think it's easier to hate than to love, he thought to himself bitterly. *At least that way you don't get hurt.*

eight

in the grotto

ummer was rapidly turning to fall in Place-Beneath-the-Castle. Wind-rustled leaves faded from green to a pale yellow hue, and violet smoke shaded the morning skies. Frost crackled on rain puddles nowadays, and although just six days had passed since Arlen's father had appeared in town, it seemed as if it had happened a month before, or even longer.

The Wednesday morning following that unpleasant visitation, a courier had brought a letter from the City of Bells to Theodora's door. The girl had heard her parents talking earnestly that evening and late into the night. Try as she might, she had been unable to hear a single word they had said. Her father had risen early, as usual, on Thursday morning and had headed for the fields.

As for Arlen and Theodora, the past six days had brought forth nothing whatsoever of interest. Arlen's carefully written notes about their search for the King seemed like utter nonsense to him, and when Theodora thought and dreamed and wondered, she felt more foolish than happy. To both children, all their experiences and revelations seemed to have led up to a vast, stark silence. Thursday evening Arlen and Theodora had barely said goodbye when they parted.

But in the darkest hour of the night, all that was forever changed. Arlen awoke abruptly to the sound of pounding on Granma's cottage door. There he found Theodora shivering in her nightgown, wrapped in a quilt, and weeping. "They've taken Father away. They've taken Father away . . ." she cried over and over again.

"Who, Theodora? Who on earth would take your father?" Granma had joined Arlen at the door and was trying her best to make sense of the situation.

"Granma, it's the work of my father and the Six Cruel Kings. Theodora's father is in terrible danger. She and I will have to go help him."

"Arlen! You're just children, and it's a terribly cold night. We'll just send word for the village guardians to come and help."

"Forget about the village guardians. *We* must go, Granma. Please believe me. I know what I'm talking about! I have to help Theodora because the King sent word to me!"

"When?"

"Weeks ago. Granma, we have to go. *Now!*"

With that, Arlen ran upstairs, pulled on his clothes, and grabbed all the blankets off his bed and his notes from beneath the mattress. He and Theodora ran to her house, where they found all the brothers and sisters crying, while Theodora's mother stared silently into the fireplace ashes.

"We are going to find him, Mother." Very, very large with her unborn child, Theodora's mother simply nodded in silence. She had no idea what to say or do.

"We'll take Father's horse, and we'll be back soon. Please don't worry, Mother. Try not to worry."

Dressed as warmly as possible and shrouded in blankets, the boy and girl ran to the animal shed and untied Barley, Burke's faithful white saddle horse. Theodora had known the beast all her life and had ridden him many times seated in front of her father. Now he patiently received the burden of the two children. Sensing their urgency, he headed toward the City of Bells more quickly than either child would have imagined he could gallop.

The sky was strewn with stars, and a yellow moon hung on the horizon. The castle was barely visible. Dull and illusive, it appeared to be more a part of the pinnacles than a silver fortress.

Was it really there at all?

The children rode in silence. At first they felt excited, alert with adventure. But minutes soon turned to hours, and the road between Place and the next village was longer than Arlen remembered. Worse yet, it passed through a deep wood that seemed to close in around them. They found themselves looking up into creaky, twisted branches. Now and then the cry of a wild animal chilled their blood.

But still, they carried on. The horse was foaming with effort by now and would need a drink and a rest before long. There were still several hours before sunrise when they slowed to a trot at the first buildings of Kingsdale, the township between Place-Beneath-the-Castle and the City of Bells. They passed through the outskirts of the town, down the main street, and out the other side without incident. There they found a small stream and a sheltered rock formation next to it. They dismounted and led the horse to the water. Wrapping

themselves in blankets, they curled up on the ground to
rest for a moment or two.

       🙢 🙢 🙢

Arlen and Theodora awoke at the same time to the
sound of rushing water. At first, they thought it was coming from the stream where Barley had been drinking.
But once they opened their sleepy eyes, they found
themselves staring into the face of a rainbow messenger
who shimmered directly in front of them.

"Go now, children! And go quickly! The Children of
the South will see you and will try to stop you, but you
will be protected. Go, and do not rest until you are at
the grotto in the City of Bells."

The messenger then brought out a blue bottle
capped in silver and opened it. "Take a little of this,
each of you. It will give you strength."

The clear liquid smelled like wildflowers in the
spring wind. It tasted as sweet as fresh berries in the
summer sun and warmed them like an autumn fire.
Arlen and Theodora were not only revived, they were
suddenly filled with joy.

After the waterfall voice had ceased and the rainbow
had vanished, Barley whinnied several times and tossed
his white head. The children stood up, folded their blankets, and climbed onto his broad back once again. Ener-
gized by their sips from the blue bottle, the children suddenly wished they'd asked the messenger to give a drop
or two to Barley as well. He seemed to be moving ever
so slowly now.

*The children rode in silence. At first they felt excited,
alert with adventure.*

"Arlen, I'm so ashamed. I wanted to help my father, and then I fell asleep, as if he didn't matter a bit!"

"Don't blame yourself. We must have been more tired than we realized. I can't believe we fell asleep so quickly and slept so long. It's nearly morning, and if it hadn't been for the rainbow messenger, we'd still be dreaming!"

The brighter the sky grew, the more alarmed the children became. Would the City of Bells ever come into sight? And what would happen when the Children of the South appeared? Even though the messenger had promised protection from them, the very thought of them was dreadful, especially to Theodora.

It wasn't long before that particular question was answered. As if out of nowhere, a rock sailed over their heads, and another hit Barley's side with a thud. Fortunately, the big horse didn't seem to feel it.

"You can't hurt us! The King will deal with you!" Arlen shouted at the angry faces that peered around trees and over rocks. "The King is on our side!"

Although the rocks continued to fly, not one of them hit the children. There must have been more than two dozen of the troublesome boys and girls spread out along each side of the highway. Theodora hid her head and covered her frightened eyes. Arlen looked fiercely from left to right, having half a mind to steer the horse directly into the midst of the Children of the South just to give them a scare. He had the good sense not to, remembering the messenger's words—*"Go, and do not rest until you reach the grotto."*

Before many minutes, the City of Bells came into full sight on the horizon, the hateful children far behind.

But now another problem arose. Where was the grotto? Arlen had grown up in the city, but he had never heard of such a place. He frowned and tried to imagine what it was. It had to be the headquarters of the Six Cruel Kings, he reasoned. They were behind this evil kidnapping, and they were the true King's avowed enemies.

"I think we'll head for the south side of the city, Theodora. I've heard that the Six Cruel Kings control some of the streets there, and perhaps that's where we'll find your poor father."

"Whatever you say, Arlen. Let's just hurry. By now he could be . . ." She could not finish the sentence, so horrible was the thought that someone might actually kill him.

Meanwhile Arlen, fueled by his own hatred, frantically drove the exhausted horse. Deep inside, he determined that this adventure would bring his father to justice of some sort, and the sooner the better. Of course, in the process, they would also rescue Theodora's father.

Once the pair arrived on the rundown, south side of the city, they slowed their pace and began to look up and down the drab streets, wondering about the grotto and what they should be seeking. Now and then an aimless person wandered past, evidently homeless and lost. Theodora's eyes grew wide at the sight of such a vast, complex city. On every corner of every street, seven bells hung, small to large, in a long row.

"So that's why it's called the City of Bells!" she whispered, half to herself.

"There's an old legend that someday the King will return to the kingdom," Arlen said quietly, "and that when he comes, all the bells will ring with joy."

"What a beautiful story!"

"Yes, it is. I once got myself in a lot of trouble during a history lesson, asking too many questions about that story." Arlen chuckled a little, remembering the sharp sting of the teacher's switch on his hand.

"How are we ever going to find the grotto, Arlen? There's an old man over there, sleeping under some newspapers. Do you think he knows?"

"We aren't supposed to stop, Theodora. The messenger said not to stop until we get there."

"He said 'don't stop and *rest*.' We're stopping to *ask*. That's different!"

Arlen sighed and pulled the reins against Barley's neck. The animal, more than happy to oblige, stopped at once.

"Sir!" Arlen spoke in his most authoritative voice.

The old man, who was lying on the sidewalk fast asleep, didn't stir. Arlen dismounted, walked over, and shook him. "Sir! Wake up! Do you know where the grotto is?"

"Mmmph . . ." The aged, bearded man rubbed his face with two grimy hands and sat up very, very slowly. Arlen and Theodora twitched with impatience, trying to hurry him with their thoughts.

"The grotto," repeated Arlen. "Do you know where it is?"

"Mmmmph . . . grotto. Ah, the grotto, young lad. D'ye know the old King's Hall where they have the ceremonies?"

"Ceremonies?"

"The ceremonies, lad. The ones they used to have for the King. They still go through the same ceremonies there in the King's Hall, but they never mention his

name anymore. They think he's dead, y'know, since he's
not coming here these days."

"The grotto is where, then?" Arlen was struggling
with all his might to be understanding and patient.

"Underneath, lad, underneath the King's Hall! Next
street, you'll see the grand old building. Used to be a
great place in the early days." The old man's pale eyes
brightened with memories. "Why, yes sir, when the King
arrived, the flags would fly and the bells would ring.
He'll be back, you know, boy. Yes, he will. And those de-
ceivers will run with fear when they see his lovely face.
That they will, lad. That they will."

The old man lay back down, covered his head with
the newspaper, and fell fast asleep once again.

"Next street, and he pointed left." Arlen repeated
the words as he pulled himself onto Barley's damp back.
"Next street . . ."

They rounded a corner and found a massive stone
building at the top of a broad stone staircase. Two marble beasts framed the doorway, and seven pillars held a
magnificent carved roof. It was a ghostly looking place
which had fallen into disrepair over countless years.
Seven empty flagpoles stood in front of it, and screech-
ing black birds flew in and out between the pillars.

The children left Barley in the street (after giving
clear instructions to the faithful beast not to move an
inch until they returned) and tiptoed up the stairs, un-
consciously holding hands as they approached the heavy,
cobwebbed door that stood just ajar. It creaked loudly as
they pushed it open and peered into a cavernous, echo-
ing sanctuary.

Rows and rows of empty wooden benches lined the floor. A platform stretched across the front of the room, and a man in a red and black robe stood behind a podium there. To the children's amazement, six or eight ancient-looking men and women were seated in the front, taking part in some sort of liturgy.

"To loyalty!" the robed man's voice croaked from the platform as he lit a candle and burned something in a bronze dish.

"To loyalty!" the handful of people in the seats responded with shaky voices.

"To justice!"

"To honor!"

"This is our most honored shrine, ladies and gentlemen. And it stands as a monument to our good works and to our own honor and glory.

"And so we go in peace."

"And so we go in peace," echoed the others who were clearly paying no attention to anything they were saying. Once he concluded, they rose slowly to their feet and shuffled toward the door. The children watched the procession of withered people, bent and stiff with age, move toward them.

"Do you know where the grotto is?" Arlen asked a feeble couple.

"Downstairs, lad." The man's voice rattled as he spoke. "Where the Six meet."

Puzzled by the peculiar scene and most troubled to hear about the Six, Theodora and Arlen turned and ran, looking for a downstairs entrance. They scurried along the side of the building and finally discovered a cave-like

opening near the back. Smoke seemed to be drifting out
of it, and a dim glow lit the ground outside.

Just as they started toward it, a group of evil-faced
children rushed toward them. "You are not welcome
here, you country bumpkins!" one of them shrieked.
"This is a place of power, not a barnyard!"

"You cannot hurt us. The King has said so!" Arlen
shouted the words into the boy's face and pushed him
out of the way, tugging Theodora along by the hand. To
his surprise, the troublesome child did not follow but
seemed oddly frozen in place.

Arlen and Theodora approached the grotto opening
in great fear, shuddering as they looked inside. What
they saw through the smoky haze was far more terrifying
than anything they could possibly have imagined.

A scowling man read from a parchment scroll, which
he held between clawlike fingers. "You will be cast into
the castle pit, Burke Brighton, for refusing to obey the
orders of the Six Kings."

The reader wore a jewel-colored robe, and a thin
band of ebony circled his head. "Even though we paid
you in advance for the responsibility, you refused to stop
your daughter Theodora from searching for the enemy."

Theodora covered her face with her hands and
gasped in horror. In the torch light, she and Arlen could
just make out the form of her father, bound, gagged,
and blindfolded, his head bowed.

"And, Burke Brighton, we also remind you of your
past crimes. Do you recall how you refused to serve us,
even as a young boy? Instead, you foolishly chose to
seek the enemy. Because of this, you have a double in-

dictment against you. You will be taken to the castle pit at sunrise tomorrow. At midnight you will be thrown in."

The five bony men seated at the stone table murmured their assent.

"And you will not be alone there, Brighton. Bring in the other one."

Just then two huge, grotesque creatures dragged another prisoner into the grotto. He, too, was bound and blindfolded but was still free to speak.

"You have betrayed me!" he whined. "I served you, and you betrayed me!"

"You did not obey us, Greyton Ardourman. You did not stop your son, Arlen, from consorting with the enemy. You did not stop his friend Theodora from her childish quest. Most of all, you have not shown respect for us, your six wise counselors. You, therefore, will join this country rebel in the castle pit."

Once the kings at the table muttered their assent, the two monstrous beings shoved a rag in Greyton's mouth and tied it behind his head. As the two prisoners were led away, Theodora and Arlen fled in absolute terror from their doorway vantage point.

The boy and girl could not conceive of where, or what, the castle pit might be. They knew only that their innocent quest seemed to have come to a heartbreaking conclusion. Their fathers were sentenced to die tomorrow. And they, Arlen and Theodora, were in grave and certain danger.

In their panic and grief they did not see the rainbow beings who fiercely guarded them as they huddled together in the shadows; nor did they hear the squeals of the southern children who were roughly jerked away from them by unseen hands; nor did they feel the warmth of the King's smile as he made preparations for the favored friends who would soon be visiting him at his castle.

nine

to the
castle pit

he sentencing complete, the Grotto stood silent and empty. Theodora, weeping uncontrollably, sat with her back against a wall. Her eyes were nearly swollen shut, and both her sleeves were soaked with tears. She had reached the end of her strength, and Arlen could not even make her hear his words of comfort. What could he say to convince her that she was not personally responsible for her dear father's execution tomorrow?

Distracted by fear and half blinded by fury toward his own father, the boy pulled his notes out of his breast pocket and read them again and again. Only one sentence seemed to matter in that horrible moment: *"You must think of your friend Theodora more kindly than you think of yourself."*

He looked at the small girl and realized that neither of them had eaten or slept for many hours. Already, afternoon shadows were chilling the air, and soon night would come with its icy winds. Arlen's eyes swept the street, and to his relief, he saw Barley patiently waiting there, stomping first one foot and then another.

87

We've got to find a place to rest and maybe get something to eat, too. But where?

"Theodora, come with me." He gently pulled her by the hand. "Come on."

"I can't leave my father here, Arlen! What if they take him away, and I don't see them? We don't know where the castle pit is, and if we're going to find it, we'll have to follow them there!"

"Theodora, they won't leave until sunrise tomorrow. That's part of the sentence, remember? We'll be back well before that, and we'll be more rested and better able to help."

If there's any help to be offered, he added privately to himself.

Theodora began to cry again, but she obediently rose and walked with Arlen toward poor, thirsty Barley.

Where on earth am I going to take her? I wonder if the King knows about this. Are you watching, King? Well, maybe you can tell me what to do next!

The children climbed atop the faithful horse and headed him back toward the north side of the City of Bells. As they moved away from the grotto and the prison cells beneath it, Theodora felt as if her heart were being ripped apart. She kept looking back over her shoulder and crying, "Father, I'm so sorry . . ."

Arlen, in the meantime, felt so frightened and frustrated that he could barely concentrate on his search for a place to stay that night.

Fortunately, Barley was the one member of the party whose mind was focused on such important matters as food, drink, and rest. He plodded along, moving slower and slower, up one street and down another, until he finally came to a complete stop in front of a little wooden house. A carefully painted sign across the door read *The King's Bed and Breakfast.*

Arlen shouted at the horse, kicked him, hit the reins against him, and finally dismounted and tried to pull him along. The boy couldn't see the rainbow being who stood in front of Barley, powerfully blocking his progress. The beast refused to move a muscle.

"Arlen, look," Theodora said weakly, pointing at the sign. "Maybe we could sleep here. It says *Bed and Breakfast.*"

"You have to pay to stay in those places," Arlen explained impatiently, tugging on the horse's bridle, "and we haven't so much as a coin between us."

Theodora slid off Barley's back and walked unsteadily toward the door. "I'm going to ask, anyway." She lifted the brass knocker, not noticing that the words *Love the King* were engraved upon it.

A young woman with braided black hair opened the door, her tawny face wreathed in a radiant smile. "Yes? How may I help you?" she inquired politely, bowing a little so she could hear Theodora's reply.

"We, my friend and I," she pointed at Arlen, "are from a village named Place-Beneath-the-Castle, and we've come here looking for my father, who is lost. We have no money and no food, and we wondered if you would have a place where we could sleep until sunrise. We have to leave then."

The woman nodded, taking careful notice of Theodora's tear-stained face, wrinkled clothes, and the dark circles around her eyes. "Yes, of course. Why don't you come in? I have two empty rooms tonight and plenty of food for children. Tell me, love, does your mother know where you are?"

"Yes. She wanted me to come." Theodora was almost ready to tell the entire story to the kind woman, but Arlen, who by now had joined her in the doorway, shot her a warning look which caused her to keep still.

Within minutes, the tired children were seated at a table covered with hand-crocheted white lace and set with simple country cutlery. The woman brought them bowls of steaming soup, freshly baked, buttered bread, and goblets of sweet, red juice. Delightful smells filled the cozy house, and even Theodora, who had thought she was grieved beyond appetite, ate until she was full. After that, she even stuffed down a frosted nutcake or two.

The hostess watched the children with a quiet smile on her face. She excused herself, stabling Barley with an ample supply of oats and fresh water. She drew hot baths for each child, and while they bathed, she pressed their clothes. Less than an hour after their arrival, Arlen and Theodora had been scrubbed clean, tucked between crisp, white sheets, and had fallen sound asleep.

At their request, the woman woke them at four o'clock in the morning, fed them an enormous breakfast, and sent them away, their hopes renewed. As they left the house, Theodora noticed a needlepoint plaque on the entryway wall. *To Love Is to Serve,* it said. "Do you know the King?" she whispered to the woman, who nodded in reply.

"We very much need his help. If you have a way of letting him know about our search for my father, would you please do so?"

"I will do my best." The woman kissed each of them. "Never forget that the King feels," she smiled. "The King knows. And the King understands."

"I wish we could pay you for your courtesy," Arlen offered thankfully before they rode away.

"Seeing you rested and ready to go is thanks enough!"

Warmed by her unexpected hospitality, the children were better able to bear the sight of the vast assemblage gathering outside the grotto as they arrived. Dozens of men dressed in dark colors, carrying torches, and waiting impatiently for marching orders were standing in the street outside the King's Hall. The children watched from behind a building, where Barley had found a patch of grass and a puddle for himself.

Just as the sun appeared at the horizon, a trumpet sounded a single note, and a grim procession began. Six black, windowless coaches drawn by black steeds led the way, followed by the men in the streets, who seemed to grow in number with every passing moment. At the rear of the entourage trudged the two prisoners, their hands tied behind them, their mouths gagged. Only their blindfolds had been removed, apparently so they could fully experience the humiliation of their death march.

Six of the grotesque creatures that had guarded the grotto marched behind the prisoners, never once looking behind them. They made odd, grunting sounds as they lumbered along. Arlen and Theodora had decided to follow the hideous parade on foot, leaving Barley behind. Trembling, they set out, desperately hoping not to be noticed.

A wide highway led out of the City of Bells and turned upward, toward the mountains. Throughout the day, the children grew more and more exhausted, and the slope kept increasing. With every step the way narrowed and roughened, and it soon seemed as if they were headed for the pinnacles themselves, where the castle was supposed to be.

The castle pit . . . Arlen thought to himself. *Maybe the place of execution is somewhere near the castle!* Excitement gripped him. He watched his father's back with renewed interest. Maybe, just maybe, the foul man would be confronted with the King's justice once and for all!

As hours passed, the children's legs grew weak and sore. Their feet throbbed with pain, and their lungs gasped for air. More than once, they remembered the warm lodgings of the night before. They never would have made it this far but for the young woman's kindness.

After nearly twelve agonizing hours, the road curved sharply, and the procession stalled abruptly. Arlen and Theodora stopped, slipped behind a tree, and looked around. Woods stretched out to their left, and a rocky precipice plunged along the righthand side of the roadway. Ahead they could see a sort of meadow over which a pall of smoke and haze hung in gray clouds. And beyond that . . .

Theodora caught her breath and grabbed Arlen's arm at the same moment. "Look!"

Beyond the smoky meadow was a rocky formation, studded with hundreds of perfectly formed evergreen trees. And built upon it, as if carved from alabaster, was a huge castle, glowing pure and white against the night sky. The moon was just rising above the forest, and wherever its light spilled, the castle's slender turrets shone like purest silver.

By now the crowd had swarmed into the meadow, where men were shoving their torches in the ground and building bonfires. The children had completely lost sight of the prisoners. Arlen took Theodora's hand and led her running through the forest, closer to the clearing. As they ran, they heard voices behind them shouting, "You have no business here, you trash!" and "You stupid oafs! Go back to the farmyard!"

"It's them! The evil children! They're chasing us!" Theodora was so exhausted and so concerned about her father that she hardly cared.

"We're not to worry about them, Theodora. Just keep running."

He turned around and looked just in time to see one of the hideous giants in close pursuit, a heavy tree branch in his hands. His pounding footfalls grew nearer, and Arlen prepared himself for a painful blow. But just then, unexplainably, the creature stumbled, cried out in a guttural voice, and fell down, never to rise again.

Neither Theodora nor Arlen had yet learned that rainbow beings not only appeared as ordinary men but also became quite invisible when necessary.

At last the children reached a cluster of huge rocks, where they stopped, climbed, and peered over the top. Once they saw what was on the other side, it was all they could do not to cry out. Their fathers, tied to slender saplings, stood less than ten paces away. Fires blazed all around them, and past the flames the children could see a vast, smoking pit.

"So that's what the castle pit is—it's something like a volcano, I think."

"A what?"

"A volcano is a mountain with fire inside, Theodora. See? That's where they are going to throw your father— and mine, of course," he added with some satisfaction.

The children withdrew and tried to develop a plan. In the moonlight, Arlen could hardly make out his notes. The only words he could read were *Those who love must forgive.*

Forgive! I will never forgive my father! He raged and cursed at the man who stood bound and pitiful just across the stone barrier from him. The boy was paralyzed with hatred, and thoughts of past cruelties repeated themselves in his mind again and again.

Theodora, in the meantime, was lost in tender memories of her own father. She remembered resting in his arms, her head against his chest. She recalled the warmth of his face when she kissed it and the strength of his arms as he lifted her onto his shoulders to carry her across the fields back home. Her heart swelled with loving remembrance.

I've got to do something, she thought. *I've come this far, and I'm not going to stop now.* With a sudden burst of courage, the girl scrambled back up the rocks, and before Arlen could stop her, she was climbing down the other side.

"Theodora, no!" Arlen's hoarse whisper never reached her ears. She scampered down the boulders and ran to her father's side.

"Father! I'm here! I'm going to help you! Don't be afraid! I love you, and I'm right here."

The poor man's eyes opened, and he looked at the child as if he were dreaming. Tears poured down his face, and a flicker of hope returned to his heart, at least for the moment.

For some reason, neither the Six Cruel Kings, who were now standing together talking, nor the massive throng of men caught sight of the little girl. She kissed her father's purple hands, which were tied too tightly behind his back, and then she struggled back up the rocks.

"You stupid . . ." Arlen's rage toward his father almost caused him to lash out at Theodora. He caught himself, however, remembering that he was to think more kindly of her than he did of himself.

"I'm sorry, Arlen, but I had to let him know I was here. Besides, nobody saw me. But what are we going to do now?"

"I just want to see my father suffer, that's all." The boy was scowling and seething, unable to think about anything else.

"But what about *my* father? I thought you came to help *him!*" Theodora was frightened by Arlen's rage, which had all but changed him into a stranger.

"Just sit here a minute, Theodora. I'll look at my notes again."

But alas, his notes were meaningless, so preoccupied was he with thoughts of vengeance, bitterness, and unforgiveness.

And as for Theodora, she sat weeping among the boulders, with nothing on her mind but running back to her father's side—embracing him, untying his cold hands, and kissing his rough whiskers again. She spoke aloud, her voice lost in the roar of the crowd below.

"King, are you there in the castle? Are you listening, King? You're going to have to help me because Arlen's too upset to think straight. And all I can do is sit here and cry.

"I'm sorry, King, I'm really sorry. But, you see, I'm about to lose my father. And sometimes . . . sometimes, when I really think about it, I almost wish I'd never tried to find you in the first place!

"I'm sorry, but that's the way I feel right now."

TEN

TALES
OF THE KING

n the hours between nine and midnight, the castle gleamed brighter and brighter in the moonlight. Its brilliant silver made the children's eyes ache when they looked at it, and its light clearly illuminated Arlen's tattered, worthless notes.

"What are we going to do? Couldn't we somehow cut the cords around their hands?"

"With what, Theodora? We have no knives, nothing sharp. I should have thought to bring something."

Arlen was feeling extremely useless by now, for Theodora had dashed back and forth countless times in the past three hours to encourage her father, and he had done nothing but sit and stare.

There's a castle all right, he told himself with a sneer, *but who cares? What good is a King, anyway, if he does nothing but watch the good people die with the bad?*

Theodora had been gazing at the castle herself, but her thoughts took on a very different tone. *Oh, King! Maybe you really are inside there, and maybe you really do feel and know and understand. Can you see us here? Can you see my father? You've helped us before, but now we really need your help. Please do something, because there's nothing we can do for ourselves.*

In spite of everything—the helplessness, the sorrow, and the nearness of midnight—the unspoken words made Theodora feel strangely quiet inside. She'd done all she could do, and her father was still destined to die. But she had shown him her love and even risked her life for him. That was almost enough.

Almost, but not quite.

As the moon soared high into a starless heaven, the crowd in the meadow began to stir in anticipation of the executions. The children pulled themselves up on the rocks and watched in revulsion as four horrible creatures roughly slashed away the cords that tied Greyton and Burke's numbed hands to the saplings. One beast on either side, they pushed the men along toward the edge of the smoky, fire-rimmed pit. The prisoners stood with their heads bowed, silhouetted in the eerie red glow, waiting to be thrown in.

The Six Cruel Kings marched forward haughtily, their spokesman carrying a huge, ornate parchment scroll. The old man's robe glinted amethyst in the fire-light as he began to read in a pitiless voice:

> For the first time in countless years, a death sentence has been passed against a citizen of the kingdom— and not just one citizen, but two.
>
> For the first time since the demise of the former corrupt King, we have chosen to dispose of evildoers, establishing our Wise Counsel of Six as the true defenders of the kingdom's great constitution, which states: "Those who rebel or defy the rightful ruler shall most surely die in the castle pit."
>
> It is now midnight, and we therefore declare . . .

The four hideous beasts tensed their long arms,
awaiting the final words which would permit them to
cast the two cringing prisoners into the fire. The five remaining kings stood in regal glory, waiting for their co-
hort to conclude his statement.

The silent crowd stirred impatiently in the torch
light, anxious to hear the agonized cries of Burke Brighton and Greyton Ardourman as they burned alive.

Meanwhile, Arlen and Theodora watched in breath-
less wonder, for something else was taking place right
before their eyes that would transform their lives forever.

In the midst of the fierce, angry gathering, seven
rainbow beings suddenly materialized, shimmering in
the night, their brilliance almost blinding. In a single
voice, like raging flood waters, they said but one word:
"Enough."

The children glanced at the castle, instantly aware
that the drawbridge was down and that hundreds of
other smaller beings stood along the walls, lining the par-
apets and surrounding the entire fortress with shining,
dancing color.

No one moved—not the kings, not the gruesome
creatures, not the prisoners, not the crowd—for advanc-
ing toward them, in the most magnificent robes of
gleaming white, was a man whose face disclosed sorrow
and compassion, his eyes reflecting wonder and wisdom.

"Release the prisoners," he ordered the ugly guards
in a quiet voice. "Their penalty has already been paid."

Six kings stared at his white-robed splendor. Six
faces distorted into horrible masks of hatred. Six robes
once bright with jewels now faded into drabness beside

him. Six bent bodies appeared warped and deformed in his stately presence.

"What do you mean, their penalty has been paid, you usurper!" A squawking voice from one of the kings broke the silence, and soon everyone in the entire gathering was shouting or muttering.

When the true King spoke, all fell silent again. "When I allowed you Six Cruel Kings to kill me, I proved that love is more powerful than hate, for I came back to life."

"You're a ghost, that's all, a ghost!" they shrieked, but the King ignored their accusation and continued.

"My death also removed the death penalty from the kingdom. Perhaps you have forgotten that the ancient law states, 'If a king wishes to give his life for his people, the people will not need to die for their own crimes.'"

"You didn't wish to die! We killed you in battle!"

"I knew I would live again, so I *allowed* you to take my life." The King smiled a little as he told the six men what they already knew all too well. "The love in my heart brought me back, even though you've denied it for years. So you see, no matter what you say or think, these two men must be released."

"But they are guilty!"

"Yes, they are. One is guilty because he intentionally broke the law. The other is guilty because he made a mistake. Nevertheless, both must be released. No matter how the rules are broken, the law remains the same. I have died so they can live. Therefore I command you— *release them now.*"

The King's authority was irresistible. The creatures threw their two prisoners toward him and fled in terror.

The Six Cruel Kings ran behind them, tripping awk-
wardly over their robes. Most of the men in the meadow
scattered in fright, heading back toward the City of Bells
as fast as their legs could carry them. A few lingered,
however, amazed at the sight of a living King who really
did live in the castle after all.

He spoke to these remaining few in a friendly, gentle voice. "Go on back and tell your friends and families
you've seen me. Tell them I'll be coming back into the
city one of these days. You'll know I've returned when
you hear the bells ringing!"

"And now, as for you!" All at once he turned toward
the rocks where Theodora and Arlen were hiding. His
face lit up with a warm, happy smile. "Come down here
at once!"

The children looked at each other in absolute shock.
With their astonished fathers watching, they climbed
down the rocks and tried to walk toward the King.
Numbed by his appearance, they were unable to take a
single step.

And so he went to them. He bent down and embraced
each one gently. "Welcome, Theodora. I hope by the time
you leave, you'll find reason enough to love me."

"I already love you, sir," she whispered. "How could
anyone not love you?"

"Do you know why you love me?"

She gazed at him, wondering what he meant.

"You love me because I love you, Theodora. That's
the way it always happens."

As the two were speaking, Theodora's father approached them. "Sir, kind sir," Burke began, a bit
tongue-tied, rubbing his sore hands together, "can you

ever forgive me for not telling her about you when she asked? I used to know you myself, you remember? I just got busy and forgot what you meant to me as a boy. I'm so sorry . . ."

"Burke, that's why you're standing here alive, because I've forgiven you. You're invited to the castle, all of you. I have a lot to tell you. But that reminds me . . . Arlen?"

Arlen stood stiff and scared and alone. "Yes, sir?"

"What's wrong, son? You look completely miserable, even though you've seen me at last! Are you so disappointed?"

Arlen shook his head sadly. "I'm not disappointed in you, your majesty. I'm disappointed in myself. You know I failed to do what you asked, sir. I was so angry and full of hate for my father that I couldn't do a thing to help Theodora. I'm sorry, but I just couldn't forgive him."

"Greyton, come over here." The King turned toward Arlen's father, who cowered in the shadows like a frightened animal. The disgraced man was speechless.

"Greyton, you've known of my existence all your life, but your pride and desire for power have caused you to serve the six liars. Now I'll give you one more opportunity. Either you can serve me and content yourself with *my* power and authority, or you can go back to your home right now and deny that any of this ever happened. Remember, however, that once you die, you will pay a different and far more severe penalty for refusing to serve me."

Arlen watched Greyton struggling to decide between present humility and future horror. For the first time in his young life, the boy felt a stirring of pity for his father. Finally, to everyone's sorrow, Greyton slowly turned and headed back toward the City of Bells. They all watched him go, his wavering steps barely moving him forward.

"Pride is a tragic thing, Arlen." The King put his arm around the boy's shoulders. "And I need to tell you something else: it's pride that keeps you from forgiving people. Did you know that?"

"It's hard to forgive unkind people. It's easier to treat them the way they deserve to be treated."

"Treating people the way they deserve to be treated is my business, not yours. I'm the King, and it's important for you to allow me to accomplish things in my own way and in my own time. You can't punish people with unforgiveness, anyway. It doesn't work."

"Is that why you sent the choir?" Theodora had been listening carefully.

By now the King, Arlen, Theodora, and Burke Brighton had crossed the drawbridge. Try as they might to concentrate on the castle's opaque alabaster walls, rich carpets, and immense hallways, the visitors could think of nothing but the King. Just walking beside him filled them with an inexpressible joy they'd never known before.

"I sent the choir for two reasons. I knew you, Theodora, wanted to hear more about me. Since they had just left the castle, I thought you'd be interested in what they had to say.

"And Arlen, I also knew that you needed to be warned about unforgiveness. It's like poison, you know. Look what happened today when you tried to help your friend. You were of no use to her because of the unforgiveness in your heart."

By now Arlen's hatred for his father was shrinking
into a mere twinge of sad regret. After a few more moments in the King's presence, it had vanished forever.

"I know you have lots of questions, all of you. But why
don't we talk about them during dinner? I have something
important to give you afterwards, before you leave."

They could hardly see all the way to the top of the gi-
gantic dining hall. Heavy wooden beams, suspended at
dizzying heights, arched mightily above their heads.
Countless colorful flags, hung row upon row from the
rafters, bore curious symbols and unreadable words.

"Where are they from?" Arlen, who had always en-
joyed studying heraldry, didn't recognize a single banner.

"From all the kingdoms that serve me."

Thousands of candles, dripping wax of every hue,
blazed in the alcoves that were carved into the walls.
Twelve dark-haired, bronzed men and women came in
bearing platters laden with fruits and breads and cheeses
unlike any the visitors had ever seen before.

"These men and women have brought foods for you
from their distant, seaside country. Perhaps some day I
will allow you to see for yourself a land where there is
no winter, and where the summer only fades for a few
hours at a time, when the fragrant rains fall."

"I can't imagine such a place, sir." Arlen looked ad-
miringly into the deep, dark eyes of the foreigners, who
wore garments woven of leaves and flowers.

Theodora, however, was too full of questions to be
distracted by faraway places. "Your majesty, why
couldn't we find the workman and the old woman when
we wanted to?"

"Theodora, the workman was there to tell you about my ability to heal. Your mother was soon to be ill, and I wanted you to tell me about her sickness so I could send help. The woman with the churn was there to help you become a willing servant, because service is difficult for you."

"Like forgiveness is difficult for me?" Arlen looked sympathetically at Theodora.

"Everyone has difficulty with something, and I speak in different ways to different people. You won't all hear the same messages, and you won't all learn the same lessons."

"Who were those strange people in the King's Hall, and what were they doing there?"

The King sighed, shook his head, and smiled appreciatively at the children. "It will be hard for you to understand, since you have searched so diligently for me. But for years, those people have carefully acted out the ceremonies that used to take place when I actually reigned in the King's Hall. Unfortunately, they've taken my name out of their rituals and substituted their own names instead. The truth is, they've forgotten all about me!"

Burke Brighton hadn't said a word during the meal. Amazed at the uniqueness of each taste and texture, he had sampled nearly every food on the table. He had listened and learned and longed to hear more. Now, at last, he had a question of his own.

"Sir, when they killed you, and when you came back to life, why didn't you return to the kingdom and set the record straight? Why did you let things go so long and allow the lies about you to spread? It's made things difficult for all of us, if you don't mind my saying so."

"I have been waiting and watching to see who would believe in my existence without seeing me. You yourself know how difficult that can be, Burke. But that way, when I return, I will already know who my real subjects are. And that brings up another very important matter."

He spoke a few words in another language to one of the maidens. She nodded and, with her companions, began to clear the table. "Thank you for sharing your food with us!" Theodora smiled.

"To love is to serve," a young man responded with a bow.

"Burke," the King said, "you need to return home right now. Your wife, Nan, is about to have her baby, and she's feeling lost and alone without you. I'll have one of my messengers escort you. Please assure Nan that Arlen and Theodora will return shortly."

Burke jumped to his feet, his face aglow with the thought of his coming child and his beloved Nan. He kissed Theodora goodbye, shook Arlen's hand, and hurried toward the door, the King at his side. They embraced warmly as he left, and Theodora proudly heard him say, "I'll be your man in Place. You can count on me, sir."

Once Burke had left, the King motioned for the children to join him. He led them into a towering throne room, hung floor to ceiling with colorful tapestries which seemed to depict the histories of many lands. Some of them were beautifully finished, while others appeared to be in various stages of completion.

Then the King brought forth something far more wonderful than the tapestries. It was a golden book, printed on fine, gilt-edged parchment. Once the book was opened, its pages throbbed with action. The children watched men, women, boys and girls moving through cities and villages, acting out weddings and wars, experiencing festivals and funerals. Rapidly changing scenes of life and death spoke of the King's plans, the King's gifts, and the King's wisdom.

On the cover of the book were carved but four words: *Tales of the King.*

"These are the histories of all my kingdoms, children. When those who believe in my existence study this miraculous book, they will see its pages become reality before their eyes. You have seen it yourselves. Those who don't believe will see only words—and boring, empty words at that."

"It's a wonderful book, sir."

"It is wonderful, to be sure. And I am giving it to you." He placed the book in Theodora's trembling hands. "I want you to take it back to the kingdom and show it to the people. Some will long for it. Some will avoid it. Some will dispute it. And some, like your father, Arlen, will try with all their might to destroy it. But this is my gift to the kingdom, and I am placing it in your young hands."

"Why us?" Theodora couldn't take her eyes off the vivid, lifelike words that turned into fascinating pictures every time she looked at them.

"Because you love me, Theodora. And because you obey me, Arlen. I'm sending the two of you together, to bring my stories to the kingdom."

"Why don't you take the book yourself?"

"I've decided to watch just a bit longer to see who will come to believe, Arlen. Once I return, bells will ring, songs will be sung again, and all the lessons will already have been learned."

"How long will it be?" Theodora could hardly wait.

"Sooner than you think, and longer than you wish. But tell me, children, will you do as I ask?"

"We will!" they spoke as one, and the three laughed together at the enthusiastic response. The King looked like a young man, such joy radiated from his face.

"You are such delightful children! How I hate to see you go! But the time has come. I'm sending you to-gether, with my book, my blessings, and my messengers at your side." At that very moment, Arlen and Theodora saw two rainbow beings shimmering in the throne room, ready to escort them home.

"Oh, and by the way," the King added, brushing a strand of Theodora's long hair back from her face, "in case you were wondering, you'll find your horse, Barley, safe and sound in your father's animal shed."

"How did you know I was worried? Oh, I do love you, Your Majesty! And thank you for loving me." Theodora's eyes were full of happy tears as she held him tightly in her arms and then waved goodbye.

Arlen shook the King's hand and hugged him gratefully.

And so, at last, the rainbow beings bore them in their arms on a breathtaking ride across the sky from the pinnacles to Place-Beneath-the-Castle. Despite the fact that the wind was cool in his face and the countryside spread out below him like a miniature world, Arlen frowned earnestly. He was concentrating on his new re-sponsibilities. He was planning a strategy to take the King's book to every home in Place, then to Kingsdale, and finally to the City of Bells. From there, he would have to determine what other villages and towns and cit-ies he and Theodora would need to visit. He decided to

*"I'm sending the two of you together,
to bring my stories to the kingdom."*

start writing a list of ways they could present the book to the people. He would begin the moment he arrived in Granma's cottage.

But as for Theodora, she clutched the golden book in her hands, her brown eyes soft with dreams. She thought about the King's face, the King's words, and the King's love for her.

And she dreamed of the day when she would see him again. And she wondered how long it would be until then.

ABOUT
the author

ela Gilbert is a free-lance writer living in South Laguna Beach, California. An author, collaborator, and ghostwriter, she has written or co-written more than twenty published books since 1985. She also writes poetry and music.

Along with her writing assignments, she participates in several ongoing humanitarian projects, including her work and travels with the African Children's Choir. She has two sons, Dylan David and Colin Keith, and attends St. James Episcopal Church in Newport Beach, California.

The typeface for the text of this book is *Caledonia* which was created by the talented type and book designer, William Addison Dwiggins. Dwiggins, who became acting director of the Harvard University Press in 1917, was also known for his work with the publisher Alfred Knopf and for his other type designs, notably *Electra*. The name *Caledonia* is the ancient name for what is now the country of Scotland and denotes that the type was originally designed to parallel *Scotch Roman* (sometimes described as a *Modernized Old Style*). In creating *Caledonia*, Dwiggins was also influenced by the type that William Martin cut in 1790 for William Bulmer. Thus *Caledonia* is a modification of *Bulmer* and *Scotch Roman*, yet it is more business-like and versatile than the two older types.

Substantive Editing:
Michael S. Hyatt

Copy Editing:
Peggy Moon

Cover Design:
Steve Diggs & Friends
Nashville, Tennessee

Page Composition:
Xerox Ventura Publisher
Linotronic L-100 Postscript® Imagesetter

Printing and Binding:
Maple-Vail Book Manufacturing Group
York, Pennsylvania

Cover Printing:
Strine Printing Company
York, Pennsylvania